ISBN 978-1-331-35767-4
PIBN 10178862

This book is a reproduction of an important historical work. Forgotten Books uses
state-of-the-art technology to digitally reconstruct the work, preserving the original format
whilst repairing imperfections present in the aged copy. In rare cases, an imperfection in
the original, such as a blemish or missing page, may be replicated in our edition. We do,
however, repair the vast majority of imperfections successfully; any imperfections that
remain are intentionally left to preserve the state of such historical works.

Forgotten Books is a registered trademark of FB &c Ltd.
Copyright © 2017 FB &c Ltd.
FB &c Ltd, Dalton House, 60 Windsor Avenue, London, SW19 2RR.
Company number 08720141. Registered in England and Wales.

For support please visit www.forgottenbooks.com

1 MONTH OF
FREE
READING

at
www.ForgottenBooks.com

By purchasing this book you are eligible for one month membership to ForgottenBooks.com, giving you unlimited access to our entire collection of over 700,000 titles via our web site and mobile apps.

To claim your free month visit:

www.forgottenbooks.com/free178862

"But the Great Head rocks didn't hear."

[Page 99.]

THE MAKER OF
OPPORTUNITIES

BY

GEORGE GIBBS

AUTHOR OF "THE FORBIDDEN WAY,"
"THE BOLTED DOOR," ETC.

ILLUSTRATED BY

EDMUND FREDERICK

NEW YORK AND LONDON

D. APPLETON AND COMPANY

1912

LIST OF ILLUSTRATIONS

THE
MAKER OF OPPORTUNITIES

CHAPTER I

IT was two o'clock. Mr. Mortimer Crabb
pushed back the chair from his breakfast tray and languidly took up the
morning paper. He had a reputation (in
which he delighted) of dwelling in a Castle
of Indolence, and took particular pains that
no act of his should belie it. There were persons who smiled at his affectations, for he had
a studio over a stable in one of the cross streets
up town, where he dawdled most of his days,
supine in his easy chair. The age was running to athletics, so Mr. Crabb in public
had become the apostle and high priest of
flaccidity. He raised a supercilious eyebrow
at tennis, drawled his disparagement of polo
and racquets and recoiled at the mere

mention of college football. But those highest in Crabb's favor knew that there were evenings when he met professional pugilists at this same shrine of æstheticism, who, at liberal compensation, matched their skill and heft to his.

Nor was he a mean antagonist in conversation. For Mr. Crabb had a slow and rather halting way of making the most trenchantly witty remarks, and a style exactly suited to the successful dinner table. And when a satiated society demanded something new it was to Crabb they turned for a suggestion. Mrs. Ryerson's Gainsborough ball, Jack Burrow's remarkable ushers' dinner, and the pet-dog tea at Mrs. Jennings' country place were fantasies of the mind of this *Prester* John of the effete. When to these remarkable talents is added a yacht and a hundred and fifty thousand a year, it is readily to be seen that Mr. Mortimer Crabb was a person of consequence, even in *N*ew York.

Mr. Crabb scanned the headlines of the

2

Sun, while McFee fastened his boots. But his eye fell upon an item that made him sit up straight and drop his monocle.

"H—m!" he muttered in a strange tone. "So Dicky Bowles is coming home!"

He peered at the item again and read, frowning.

"Owing to the necessity for the immediate departure of the prospective groom for Europe, the marriage of Miss Juliet Hazard, daughter of Mr. Henry Hazard, to Mr. Carl Geltman will take place on Wednesday, June twentieth, instead of in October, the month at first selected."

Crabb's expression had suddenly undergone a startling change, unknown in the *Platonic* purlieus of the Bachelors' Club. The brows tangled, the lower jaw protruded, while the feet which had languidly emerged from the dressing-room a few moments before, had partaken suddenly of the impulses which dominated the entire body. He rose abruptly and took a few rapid turns up and down the room.

"So! They didn't dare wait! *Poor* little Julie! There ought to be better things in store for her than that! And Dicky won't be here until Thursday morning! It's too evident—the haste."

He dropped into his chair, picked up the paper again, and re-read the item. June twentieth! And to-day was Sunday, June seventeenth! Geltman had taken no more chances than decency demanded. Crabb remembered the calamitous result of Hazard's ventures in Wall Street, and it was common gossip that, had it not been for Carl Geltman, the firm of Hazard and Company would long since have ceased to exist. It was easy to read between the lines of the newspaper paragraph. Between the ruin of her father's fortunes and her own, duty left Juliet Hazard no choice. And here was Dicky Bowles upon the ocean coming back to claim his own. It was monstrous.

Mr. Crabb laid aside the paper and paced the floor again. *Then* walked to the window

4

and presently found himself smiling down upon the hansom tops.

"The very thing," he said. "The very thing. It's worth trying at any rate. Jepson will help. And what a lark!" And then aloud:

"McFee," he called, "get me a hansom."

Mr. Carl Geltman sat in his office of chamfered oak, and smiled up at a photograph upon his desk, conscious of nothing but the dull ecstasy which suffused his ample person and blinded him to everything but the contemplation of his approaching nuptials. The watch-chain stretched tightly between his waistcoat pockets somehow conveyed the impression of a tension of suppressed emotions, which threatened to burst their confines. His rubicund visage exuded delight, and his short fingers caressed his blond mustache. It was difficult for him to comprehend that all of his ambitions were to be realized at once. Money, of course, would buy almost anything in New York, but Mr. Geltman had hardly dared to dream of this. Until he had seen Miss Hazard he had never even thought of marriage. After he had seen her he had thought of nothing else.

After working late in his office, Geltman dined alone at a fashionable restaurant in a state of beatitude, then lit his cigar and walked forth into Broadway for a breath of air before going to bed. The sooner to sleep, the sooner would his wedding day dawn. But the glare of the lights distracted him, the bells jangled out of harmony with his mood, so he sought a side street and walked on toward the river, where he could continue his dreams in quiet, until the hurrying thoroughfare was far behind.

He had reached a spot between tall warehouses or factories when he felt himself seized from behind by strong arms, and before he could make an outcry something soft was thrust into his mouth and he had a dim sense of sudden darkness, of hands not too tender lifting him into a carriage, a brief whispered order, a hurried drive, more carrying, the sound of lapping water and ship's bells, the throbbing of ferry paddles, the motion of a boat, and the damp night air of the river through his thin evening clothes.

When Geltman opened his eyes it was to fix them rather dully upon the deck-beams of a yacht. The rushing water alongside sent rapid reflections dancing along their polished surfaces. At first it occurred to him that he was on an ocean steamer. Had he been married, and was this—? He looked around. *No.* He was a good sailor, but the vessel rolled and pitched sharply in a way to which he was unaccustomed. He arose to a sitting posture and tried to piece together the shattered remnants of his recollection. He felt strangely stupid and inert. How long had he been lying in the bunk? He remarked that he was attired very properly in pajamas—very fine pajamas they were, too, of silk such as he wore himself. Upon the leather-covered bench opposite was a suit of flannels carefully folded,

7

white canvas shoes, stockings upon the deck, and other unfamiliar undergarments disposed upon hooks by the cabin door.

He rose suddenly, his mind dully trying to grasp the situation. He lurched to the porthole and looked out. It was a wilderness of amber-color and white, rather bewildering and terrifying seen so near at hand, for Geltman had been accustomed to look upon the ocean from the security of fifty feet of free-board. Far away where the leaping wave crests met the line of sky, he could just distinguish the faint blue of the land. He was seized with a sudden terror and, turning, he ran to the cabin door and tried to open it. It was locked. He threw himself against it and cried aloud, but his voice was lost in the rush of wind and water without. His despairing eye at this moment lit upon a push-button by the side of the bunk. He touched it with his finger and anxiously waited. There was no sound. He sat upon the edge of the bunk, conscious of a cold wind blowing upon his

8

bare toes and of a dull ache within which pro-claimed the lack of food or drink, or both. He rang again and renewed his shouting. In a moment there was the sound of a key in the lock, the door opened, and a sober, smooth-shaven person in brass buttons stood in the door.

"Did you ring, sir?" said the man, respect-fully.

"I did," said Geltman, wrathfully.

"Yes, sir," said the man. "Can I get you anything, sir?"

"Can you get me—?" began the bewildered Geltman. "Is there anything you *can't* get me? Get me some food—my own clothes—and get me—get me—out of this. Where am I? What am I doing here?"

"You were sleeping, sir," said the man, im-perturbably. "I thought you might not wish to be disturbed."

Geltman looked around him again as though unwilling to credit the evidence of his senses. He saw that the man kept his hand upon the door and eyed him narrowly.

"I've been drugged and shanghaied. What boat is this? Where are we?"

"We're at sea, sir," said the man, quietly. "Off Fire Island, I believe, sir."

"Fire Island," he cried, "and this—" as memory came back with a horrible rush— "what day is this?"

"Wednesday, June the twentieth," replied the man, calmly.

Geltman raised his hands toward the deck beams and sank upon the bunk on the verge of collapse. He remembered now—it was his wedding day!

CHAPTER II

AS the fog upon his memory still hung heavily he raised his head toward the man at the door of the cabin. That person was eyeing him rather pityingly and had come a step forward into the room.

"Shall I be getting you something, sir?" he was saying again.

Geltman sprang unsteadily to his feet.

"No," he cried. "I'm going to get out of this."

"In pajamas, sir?" said the man, reproachfully.

Geltman glanced down at the flimsy silk garment.

"Yes—in pajamas," he cried, hotly. And with an imprecation he strode past the outraged servant and rushed through the saloon and up the companion. As he raised his head and shoulders above the deck he was imme-

diately aware of a chill wind which was singing sharply through the rigging. A gentleman, in a double-breasted suit and yachting
cap, was standing aft steadying a telescope toward a distant schooner. By his side was a
short and very stocky man with a bushy red
beard and brass buttons.

"What is the meaning of this outrage?" he
cried, wildly addressing the man in the yachting cap. "Are you the owner of this yacht?"

The gentleman calmly lowered his telescope,
passed it to the bearded man, turned mildly
toward the tousled apparition and looked at
him from top to toe while the sportive wind
gleefully defined Geltman's generous figure.

"I say, old man," he said, smiling, "hadn't
you better get into some clothes?"

"C—clothes be——" chattered Geltman.
"I've been drugged, kidnapped, and shang-
haied! Somebody's going to smart for this.
Who are you? What does it mean?"

The enraged brewer, with his arms waving,
his slender garment flapping, his inflamed

countenance and ruffled hair, presented the wildest appearance imaginable. The man in the yachting cap wore an expression of commiseration and exchanged a significant glance with the red-bearded man.

"There now," said he, raising a protesting hand, "we're all your friends aboard here. You're in no danger at all, except—" he smiled at the brewer's costume—"except from a bad cold."

"What does this outrage mean?" cried Geltman anew. "You'll suffer for it. As long as I have a dollar left in the world——"

"You really don't mean that," said the gentleman. "Go below now, that's a good fellow, get breakfast and some clothes."

"No, I'll n—not," said the brewer in chilly syncopation. "I'm Carl **Geltman**, of Henry **Geltman** and Company, and I want an explanation of this outrage."

The two men exchanged another look, and the red-bearded one tapped his forehead twice with a blunt forefinger.

"I haven't the least idea what you're talking about, Mr. Fehrenbach," said the man in the yachting cap, calmly.

"Fehrenbach!" cried the brewer. "My name isn't Fehrenbach!" he screamed. "Otto Fehrenbach is on the East Side. I'm on the West. My name is Geltman, I tell you!"

The man in blue looked gravely down at the astonished brewer and pushed a bell on the side of the cabin skylight.

"*T*hat was one of the symptoms, Weckerly," he said aside to the man with the red beard.

"Yes, Doctor," said the other quizzically. "The sea air ought to do him a lot of good."

Geltman, now bewildered, limp and very much alarmed, suffered himself to be led shivering below by the two blue-shirted sailormen. There he found the steward in the cabin with a drink, and the blue flannels, and a boy laying a warm breakfast in the saloon. He dressed. At table he discovered an appetite which even his troubled spirit had not abated. Hot coffee and a cigar completed his rehabilitation. His situation would have been an agreeable joke had it not been so tragic. He had learned enough to feel that he was powerless, that there had been some terrible mistake, and that the only way out of the difficulty was through the somewhat tortuous and sparsely buoyed channels of diplomacy.

But he walked out upon deck with renewed confidence. It was early yet. If he could persuade his host of his mistake there was still time to run in shore where the telegraph might set all things right. The man in the yachting cap was smoking a pipe in the lee of the after hatch.

"Will you please tell me your name?" began the brewer, constrainedly.

"With all the good will in the world," said the other, rising. "I'm glad you're feeling better. I'm Doctor *Norman* Woolf of New York, and this," indicating the red-bearded man, "is Captain Weckerly of the *Pinta.* Captain Weckerly—Mr. Fehrenbach."

Geltman started at the repetition of the name, but he gave no other sign.

"Would you mind," said the brewer, "telling me how I came aboard your boat?"

"Not at all," said Woolf, easily. "You see, when I cruise on the *Pinta* I make it a point to leave all thought of my cases behind. But sometimes I break my rule, and when they told me of yours I made up my mind I should like to study you under intimate and extraordinary conditions and so——"

"Really, I don't quite follow——"

"And so I had to bring you out to the yacht on which I was just starting for a little run over to the Azores."

"The Azores!"

Dr. Woolf was smiling benignly at the unhappy brewer.

"You know," he continued, "these cases of aphasia have a peculiar interest for me. It seems such a little slipping of the cogs. What's in a name, after all? Yours is an old and honored one. The Fehrenbachs have made beer for fifty years——"

"It's a lie," shouted Geltman springing to his feet, unable longer to contain himself. "It's only thirty—and the stuff isn't fit to drink."

"Pray be calm. Don't you know that if this was to get abroad, it would hurt your business?"

"My business—the business of Geltman and Company——"

"The business of Fehrenbach and Company," interrupted Dr. Woolf sternly.

The unfortunate brewer with an effort contained himself. He knew that anger would avail him nothing. The only thing left was to listen patiently. He subsided again into his wicker chair and fastened his nervous gaze upon the distant horizon.

"It's a pleasure to see you capable of self-control. If you can, I should like you to try and tell me how you happened to begin using the name of Geltman."

How had he happened to use the name of Geltman!

"What would you say," continued the Doctor, without awaiting the answer, "if I were to tell you that I was Christopher Columbus and that Captain Weckerly here was Francisco *P*izarro or Hernandez Cortes? You'd say we were mistaken, wouldn't you? Of course you would. When you say that you're Geltman and we know you're Fehrenbach——"

"Stop!" roared the unhappy brewer, springing to his feet. "Stop, for the love of Heaven, and let me off this floating madhouse!"

"Calm yourself!"

"Calm myself! Can you not see that the whole thing is a terrible mistake? You have taken me for some one else. Last evening, I tell you, I was knocked down and drugged. Then I was carried to a boat and brought here. Look in my clothes, my handkerchiefs, my linen, you will see the monogram or initials C. G. Will not that be enough to satisfy you?"

"My dear sir, I assure you you were brought aboard in the very clothes you now wear. Even that cap was on your head. Can't you remember coming up the gangway with Captain Weckerly?" And then, half aloud, and with looks of misgivings toward the Captain, who was shaking his head, "He's worse than I supposed."

Geltman had taken off the yachting cap and there, perforated in the band, were the letters O. F. He searched his pockets and found a handkerchief with the same initials. As he did so he saw that the two men were looking at him with a expression of new interest and concern. His mind was still befogged. For the first time he really began to doubt himself, and the evidence of his belated memory. He had not heard that Otto Fehrenbach was mad. Was it possible that after all some dreadful misfortune had happened to him, Geltman? That a blow he had received in falling had

turned his mind, and that his soul had mi-
grated to the body of the hated Fehrenbach?
And if so, did the soul of Fehrenbach occupy
his body? Fehrenbach, sitting in *his* office,
directing *his* business with the shoddy
methods of the Fehrenbachs, driving *his*
horses, and perhaps—could it be that he was
at this moment marrying Juliet Hazard in
his place? The thought of it made him sick.
He was dimly conscious of some science which
dealt with these things. He had once read a
story of a happening of this kind at a German
university. He looked at these strangers before him and found himself returning in kind
their mysterious glances. Was he mad? Or
were they? Or were they all mad together?
He glanced aloft at the swaying masts. And
the yacht, too? Was it real or was that, too,
some fantasy of a diseased imagination?
The *Fliegende Holländer* flitted playfully
into his mind. Just forward of the cabin a
group of sailors were standing looking at him
and whispering. It was uncanny. Were they,

too, in the same state as the others? It could not be. The vessel was real. Geltman or Fehrenbach—he, himself, was real. *T*here must be some one aboard the accursed craft who would listen to him and understand. Bewildered, he walked forward. As he did so the group of sailor-men dissolved and each one hurried about some self-appointed task. He walked over to a man who was coiling a rope.

"I say, my man," he said, "are you from New York?".

"Yes, sir," said the man, but he looked over his shoulder to right and left as though seeking a mode of escape.

"Did you ever happen to drink any of Geltman's beer?"

The man gave the brewer one fleeting look, then dropped his coil and disappeared down the fo'c's'le hatch.

The brewer watched the retreating figure with some dismay. He walked toward another man who was shining some bright work around the galley stovepipe. But the man saw him coming and vanished as the other had done. An old man with a gray beard sat on a ditty box at the lee rail, sewing a pair of breeches. He was chewing tobacco and scowling, but did not move as the landsman approached.

"I say, my man," began the brewer again, "did you ever drink any of Geltman's beer?"

The old man eyed him from head to foot before he answered. But there was no fear in his face—only pity—naked and undisguised.

"*N*aw," he replied, spitting to leeward. "*T*here ain't no beer in *N*' York fer me but Otto Fehrenbach's."

Geltman looked at him a moment and then turned despairingly aft. The yacht was bewitched and they were all bewitched with her.

CHAPTER III

"IT'S lucky Ollie Farquhar's fat," said Mortimer Crabb when Geltman was out of earshot. "It was neat, Jepson, beautifully neat. Did you ever see fish take the bait better? But he'll be coming to in a minute."

Captain Jepson was watching the bewildered brewer. "He won't get much information there," he grinned.

"It can't last much longer, though," said Crabb. "How much of a run is it to the coast?"

"About an hour, sir."

"Well, keep her on her course until eight bells. Then if he insists we'll run in and land him on the beach somewhere."

"Aye, aye, sir."

"It will soon be over now. He can't get in until to-morrow and then"—Crabb beamed with satisfaction—"and then it'll be too late. Stow your smile, Jepson. He's coming back."

Not even this complete chain of circumstantial evidence could long avail against the brisk air and sunlight. In the broad expanse between the thumb and forefinger of his right hand Geltman noted the blue of some youthful tattooing. As he saw the familiar letters doubt took flight. He *was* himself. There was no doubt of that. As he went aft again he smiled triumphantly.

"Let's be done with nonsense, Dr. Woolf," he growled. "Look at that," holding his hand before Crabb's eyes. "If I'm Otto Fehrenbach how is it that the letters C. G. are marked in my hand?"

Crabb, his arms akimbo, stood looking him steadily in the eyes.

"So," he said calmly, "you're awake at last!"

He looked at Crabb and the Captain with eyes which saw not. What he had thought of saying and doing remained unsaid and undone. With no other word he lurched heavily forward and down the companion.

"There'll be a hurricane in that quarter, Jepson, or I'm not weather wise," laughed Crabb. "We'd better run in now. There isn't much sea and the wind is offshore. We'll land him at Quogue or Westhampton. In the meanwhile, keep the tarpaulin over the for'ard boat so that he can't see the name on her. We'll use the gig. If he tries to peep over the stern we'll clap him in the stateroom. It will mean five years at least for me if he learns the name of the *Blue Wing*. So look sharp, Jepson, and keep an eye on him."

"Never fear," said the Captain with a grin, and walked forward.

Crabb walked the deck in high jubilation. He looked at his watch. Three o'clock! If McFee had followed his instructions Dicky Bowles and Juliet Hazard were man and wife. He had nicely figured his chances. To Geltman he was Dr. Woolf. To his crew he was Mr. Crabb taking an unfortunate relative for an airing; to Dicky Bowles he was the rescuer of forlorn damsels and the trump of good fellows.

Crabb was fully prepared to carry the villainy through to the end. Of one thing he was certain, the sooner his guest was off the *Blue Wing* and safely landed the better.

And so, when at last Geltman came on deck with the watchful Weckerly at his heels, Crabb noted the chastened expression upon the brewer's face with singular satisfaction.

"I'll go ashore, if you please," he said, quietly.

Crabb affected disappointed surprise.

"Here? Now?" he said. "We're pretty far down the coast. *T*hat's Quogue in there. I can't very well run back to New York, but ——"

"Put me ashore, sir," said Geltman sulkily.

When the gig was lowered, Crabb bowed the brewer over the side, his evening clothes tied in a paper package.

"Good-by," said Crabb. "When you're

done with the flannels, Mr. Geltman, send 'em
to Fehrenbach."

But Geltman had no reply. He had folded
his arms and was gazing stolidly toward the
shore. The last glimpse Crabb had of him
was when the *Blue Wing* drew offshore leaving him gesticulating wildly upon the beach in
the glow of the setting sun.

When the figure was but a speck in the distance Mortimer Crabb turned away and threw
himself wearily in his wicker chair.

"Where to now, sir?" asked Jepson.

"Oh, anywhere you like."

"Sandy Hook, sir?"

"Oh, yes," he sighed, "as well go there as
anywhere else. *N*ew York, Jepson."

*P*oor Crabb! In twenty-four hours he was,
if anything, more bored than ever. The sight
of the joyous faces of Dicky Bowles and his
bride had done something to relieve the
tedium vitæ, but he knew that their joy was
of themselves and not of him, and so he gave

them a "God bless you" and his country place on Long Island for a few weeks of honeymooning. He had even had the presumption to offer them the *Blue Wing,* but Dicky, whose new responsibilities had developed a vein of prudence, refused point blank. Crabb shrugged his shoulders.

"Suit yourselves," he laughed. "It's yours if you want it."

"And have Geltman putting you in jail?"

"Oh, *he* won't trouble me."

"How do you know?"

"I've made some inquiries. He's dropped the thing."

"Are you sure?"

"Oh, yes. He's not so thick-skinned as he looks. *T*hat story wouldn't look well in print, you know."

With an outburst of friendship, Dicky threw his arms around Crabb's shoulders and gave him a bear hug.

"I'll never forget it, Mort, never! You're the salt of the earth——"

28

"There, there, Dicky. Salt should be taken in pinches, not by the spoonful, and you've mussed my cravat! Be off with you and don't come back here until matrimony has sobered you into a proper sense of your new responsibilities to your Creator."

From the window of his apartment Crabb watched Dicky's taxi spin up the avenue in the direction of the modest boarding-house which sheltered the waiting bride, then turned with a heavy sigh and rang for McFee. Love like that never comes to the very rich. He, Mortimer Crabb, was not a sentient being, but only a chattel, an animated bank account upon which designing matrons cast envious eyes and for which ambitious daughters laid their pretty snares. *N*o, love like that was not for him—or ever would be, it seemed.

His toilet made, Crabb strolled out for the air, wondering as he often did how the people on the street could smile their way through life, while he——

A hansom passed, turned just beyond and

drew up at the curb beside him, and a voice addressed him.

"Crabb! Mortimer Crabb! By all that's lucky!"

"Ross Burnett!" said Crabb, gladly. "I thought that you were dead. Have you dropped from heaven, man?"

"*No,*" laughed Ross, "not so far, only from China."

Burnett dismissed the hansom at once and together they went to the Bachelors' Club near by, where, over a friendly glass, they gathered up the loose ends of their friendship. Crabb listened with new interest as his old friend gave him an account of what had happened in the five years which had intervened since they had last met, recalling piece by piece the unfortunate events which had led to his departure from *N*ew York, and Burnett, glad of receptive ears, rehearsed it for him.

The boy had squandered his patrimony in Wall Street. *T*hen by the grace of one of the senators from New York he obtained from the President an appointment as consular clerk, an office, which if it paid but little at home carried with it some dignity, a little authority, and certain appreciable perquisites in foreign ports.

He had chosen wisely. At Cairo, where he had been sent to fill a temporary vacancy caused by the death of the consul general and subsequent illness of his deputy, he found himself suddenly in charge of the consular office in the fullest press of business, with diplomatic functions requiring both ingenuity and discretion.

After all, it was very simple. The business of a consulate was child's play, and the usual phases in the life of a diplomat were to be requisitely met by the usages of gentility—a quality Burnett discovered was not too amply possessed by those political gentlemen who sat abroad in the posts of honor to represent the great republic.

He thought that if he could get a post,

however small, with plenary powers, he would be happy. But, alas! He had been away from home so long that he didn't even know whether his senator was dead or alive, and when he reached Washington, a month or so after the inauguration, he realized how small were his chances for preferment.

The President and Secretary of State were besieged daily by powerful politicians, and one by one the posts coveted, even the smallest of them, were taken by frock-coated, soft-batted, flowing-tied gentlemen, whom he had noticed lounging and chewing tobacco in the Willard Hotel lobby. It was apparently with such persons that power took preferment. His roseate dreams vanished. Ross Burnett was a mere State Department drudge again at twelve hundred a year!

He told Crabb that he had spoken to the chief of the diplomatic bureau in despair.

"Isn't there any way, Crowthers?" he had asked. "Can't a fellow ever get any higher?"

"If he had a pull, he might—but a consular

clerk——" The shake of Crowthers' head was eloquent.

"Isn't there anything a fellow—even a consular clerk—could do to win promotion in this service?" he continued.

Crowthers had looked at him quizzically.

"Yes, there's one thing. If you could do that, you might ask the Secretary for anything you wanted."

"And that——"

"Get the text of the treaty between Germany and China from Baron Arnim."

Crowthers had chuckled. Crabb chuckled, too. He thought it a very good joke. Baron Arnim had been the special envoy of Germany to China, accredited to the court of the Eastern potentate with the special mission of formulating a new and secret treaty between these monarchs. He was now returning home carrying a copy of this document in his baggage.

Burnett had laughed. It *was* a good joke. "You'd better send me out again," Burnett had said, hopelessly. "Anything from Arakan to Zanzibar will do for me."

Crabb listened to the story with renewed marks of appreciation.

"So you've been out and doing in the world, after all?" he said, languidly, "while we— *eheu jam satis!*—have glutted ourselves with the stale and unprofitable. How I envy you!"

Burnett smoked silently. It was very easy to envy from the comfortable vantage ground of a hundred and fifty thousand a year.

"Why, man, if you knew how sick of it all I am," sighed Crabb, "you'd thank your stars for the lucky dispensation that took you out of it. Rasselas was right. I've been pursuing the phantoms of hope for thirty years, and I'm still hopeless. *T*here have been a few bright spots"—Crabb smiled at his cigar ash—"a very few, and far between."

"Bored as ever, Crabb?"

"Immitigably. To live in the thick of things and see nothing but the pale drabs and grays. No red anywhere. Oh, for a passion

34

that would burn and sear—love, hate, fear! I'm forever courting them all. And here I am still cool, colorless and unscarred. Only once"—his gray eyes lit up marvelously—"only once did I learn the true relation of life to death, Burnett; only once. That was when the *Blue Wing* struggled six days in a hurricane with Hatteras under her lee. It was glorious. *T*hey may talk of love and hate as they will; fear, I tell you, is the *T*itan of passions."

Burnett was surprised at this unmasking.

"You should try big game," he said, carelessly.

"I have," said the other; "both beasts and men—and here I am in flannels and a red tie! I've skinned the one and been skinned by the other—to what end?"

"You've bought experience."

"Cheap at any cost. You can't buy fear. Love comes in varieties at the market values. Hate can be bought for a song; but fear, genuine and amazing, is priceless—a gem which

only opportunity can provide; and how seldom opportunity knocks at any man's door!"

"Crabb the original—the esoteric!"

"Yes. The same. The very same. And
you, how different! How sober and
rounded!"

There was a silence, contemplative, retrospective on both their parts. Crabb broke it.

"*T*ell me, old man," he said, "about your
position. Isn't there any chance?"

Burnett smiled a little bitterly.

"I'm a consular clerk at twelve hundred a
year during good behavior. When I've said
that, I've said it all."

"But your future?"

"I'm not in line of promotion."

"Impossible! *Politics?*"

"Exactly. I've no pull to speak of."

"But your service?"

"I've been paid for that."

"Isn't there any other way?"

"Oh, yes," Burnett laughed, "that treaty.
I happened to know something about it when

I was out there. It has to do with neutrality, trade ports and coaling stations; but just what, the devil only knows, and his deputy, Baron Arnim, won't tell. Arnim is now in Washington, ostensibly sight-seeing, but really to confer with Von Schlichter, the ambassador there, about it. You see, we've got rather more closely into the Eastern question than we really like, and a knowledge of Germany's attitude is immensely important to us."

"*P*ray go on," drawled Crabb.

"*T*hat's all there is. The rest was a joke. Crowthers wants me to get the text of that treaty from Baron Arnim's dispatch-box."

"Entertaining!" said Crabb, with clouding brow. And then, after a pause, with all the seriousness in the world: "And aren't you going to?"

Burnett turned to look at him in surprise. "What?"

"Get it. The treaty."

"The treaty! From Baron Arnim! You don't know much of diplomacy, Crabb."

"You misunderstood me," he said, coolly; and then, with lowered voice:

"Not from Baron Arnim—from Baron Arnim's dispatch-box."

Burnett look at his acquaintance in a maze. Crabb had been thought a mystery in the old days. He was an enigma now.

"Surely you're jesting."

"Why? It oughtn't to be difficult."

Burnett looked fearfully around the room at their distant neighbors. "But it's burglary. Worse than that. If I, in my connection with the State Department, were discovered tampering with the papers of a foreign government, it would lead to endless complications and, perhaps, the disruption of diplomatic relations. Such a thing is impossible. Its very impossibility was the one thing which prompted Crowthers' suggestion. Can't you understand that?"

Crabb was stroking his chin and contemplating his well-shaped boot.

"Admit that it's impossible," he said calmly.

"Do you think, if by some chance you were enabled to give the Secretary of State this information, you'd better your condition?"

"What is the use, Crabb?" began Burnett.

"It can't do any harm to answer me."

"Well—yes, I suppose so. If we weren't plunged immediately into war with Emperor William."

"Oh!" Crabb was deep in thought. It was several moments before he went on, and then, as though dismissing the subject.

"What are your plans, Ross? Have you a week to spare? How about a cruise on the *Blue Wing?* There's a lot I know that you don't, and a lot you know that I'd like to. I'll take you up to Washington whenever you're bored. What do you say?"

Ross Burnett accepted with alacrity. He remembered the *Blue Wing,* Jepson and Valentin's dinners. He had longed for them many times when he was eating spaghetti at Gabri's little restaurant in Genoa.

When they parted it was with a conscious-

ness on the part of Burnett that the affair of
Baron Arnim had not been dismissed. The
very thought had been madness. Was it only
a little pleasantry of Crabb's? If not, what
wild plan had entered his head? It was un-
like the Mortimer Crabb he remembered.

And yet there had been a deeper current
flowing below his placid surface that gave a
suggestion of desperate intent which nothing
could explain away. And how illimitable
were the possibilities if some plan could be de-
vised by which the information could be obtained without resort to violent measures! It
meant for him at least a post at the helm somewhere, or, perhaps, a secretaryship on one of
the big commissions.

The idea of burglary, flagrant and nefari-
ous, he dismissed at a thought. Would there
not be some way—an unguarded moment—a
faithless servant—to give the thing the aspect
of possible achievement? As he dressed he
found himself thinking. of the matter with
more seriousness than it deserved.

CHAPTER IV

A WEEK had passed since the two friends had met, and the *Blue Wing* now lay in the *P*otomac near the Seventh Street wharf. It was night and the men had dined.

Valentin's dinners were a distinct achievement. They were of the kind which made conclusive the assumption of an especial heaven for cooks. After coffee and over a cigar, which made all things complete, Mortimer Crabb chose his psychological moment.

"Burnett," he said, "you must see that treaty and copy it."

Burnett looked at him squarely. Crabb's glance never wavered.

"So you *did* mean it?" said Burnett.

"Every word. You must have it. I'm going to help."

"It's hopeless."

"Perhaps. But the game is worth the candle."

"A bribe to a servant?"

"Leave that to me. Come, come, Ross, it's the chance of your life. Arnim, Von Schlichter and all the rest of them dine at the British embassy to-night. There's to be a ball afterward. They won't be back until late. We must get into Arnim's rooms at the German embassy. Those rooms are in the rear of the house. There's a rain spout and a back building. You can climb?"

"To-night?" Burnett gasped. "You found out these things to-day?"

"Since I left you. I saw Denton Thorpe at the British embassy."

"And you were so sure I'd agree! Don't you think, old man——"

"Hang it all, Burnett! I'm not easily deceived. You're down on your luck; that's plain. But you're not beaten. Any man who can buck the market down to his last thousand the way you did doesn't lack sand. The end isn't an ignoble one. You'll be doing the Administration a service—and yourself. Why, how can you pause?"

Burnett looked around at the familiar fittings of the saloon, at the Braun prints let into the woodwork, at the flying teal set in the azure above the wainscoting, at his immaculate host and at his own conventional black. Was this to be indeed a setting for Machiavellian conspiracy?

Crabb got up from the table and opened the doors of a large locker under the companion. Burnett watched him curiously.

Garment after garment he pulled out upon the deck under the glare of the cabin lamp; shoes, hats and caps, overcoats and clothing of all sizes and shapes from the braided gray of the coster to the velvet and sash of the Niçois.

He selected a soft hat and a cap and two long, tattered coats of ancient cut and style and threw them over the back of a chair. Then he went to his stateroom and brought out a large square box of tin and placed it on the table.

He first wrapped a handkerchief around his neck, then seated himself deliberately before the box, opened the lid and took out a tray filled with make-up sticks. These he put aside while he drew forth from the deeper recesses mustachios, whiskers and beards of all shapes and complexions. He worked rapidly and silently, watching his changing image in the little mirror set in the box lid.

Burnett, fascinated, followed his skillful fingers as they moved back and forth, lining here, shading there, not as the actor does for an effect by the calcium, but carefully, delicately, with the skill of the art anatomist who knows the bone structure of the face and the pull of the aging muscles.

In twenty minutes Mortimer Crabb had aged as many years, and now bore the phiz of a shaggy rum-sot. The long coat, soft hat and rough bandanna completed the character. The fever of the adventure had mounted in

Burnett's veins. He sprang to his feet with a reckless gesture of final resolution.

"Give me my part!" he exclaimed. "I'll play it!"

The aged intemperate smiled approval. "Good lad!" he said. "I thought you'd be game. If you hadn't been I was going alone. It's lucky you're clean shaved. Come and be transfigured."

And as he rapidly worked on Burnett's face he completed the details of his plan. Like a good general, Crabb disposed his plans for failure as well as for success.

They would wear their disguises over their evening clothes. Then, if the worst came, vaseline and a wipe of the bandannas would quickly remove all guilty signs from their faces, they could discard their tatters, and resume the garb of convention.

Ross Burnett at last rose swarthy and darkly mustached, lacking only the rings in his ears to be old Gabri himself. He was fully awakened to the possibilities of the adventure.

45

Whatever misgivings he had had were speedily dissipated by the blithe optimism of his companion.

Crabb reached over for the brandy decanter.

"One drink," he said, "and we must be off."

The night was thick. A mist which had been gathering since sunset now turned to a soft drizzle of rain. Crabb, hands in pockets and shoulders bent, walked with a rapid and shambling gait up the street.

"We can't risk the cars or a cab in this," muttered Crabb. "We might do it, but it's not worth the risk. Can you walk? It's not over three miles."

It was after one o'clock before they reached Highland Terrace. Without stopping they examined the German embassy at long range from the distant side of Massachusetts 'Avenue. A gas lamp sputtered dimly under the *porte-cochère*. Another light gleamed far up in the slanting roof. Crabb led the way around and into the alley in the

46

rear. It was long, badly lighted and ran the entire length of the block.

"I got the details in the city plot-book from a real-estate man this afternoon. He thinks I'm going to buy next door. I wanted to be particular about the alleys and back entrances." Crabb chuckled.

Burnett looked along the backs of the row of *N* Street houses. They were all as stolid as sphinxes. Several lights at wide intervals burned dimly. The night was chill for the season, and all the windows were down. The occasion was propitious. The rear of the embassy was dark, except for a dim glow in a window on the second floor.

"That should be Arnim's room," said Crabb.

He tried the back gate. It was unlocked. Noiselessly they entered, closing it after them. There was a rain spout, which Crabb eyed hopefully; but they found better luck in the shape of a thirty-foot ladder along the fence.

"A positive invitation," whispered Crabb,

joyfully. "Here, Ross; in the shadow. Once on the back building the deed is done. Quiet, now. You hold it and I'll go up."

Burnett did not falter. But his hands were cold, and he was trembling from top to toe with excitement. He could not but admire Crabb's composure as he went firmly up the rungs.

He saw him reach the roof and draw himself over the coping, and in a moment Burnett, less noiselessly but safely, had joined his fellow criminal by the window. There they waited a moment, listening. A cab clattered down Fifteenth Street, and the gongs on the car line clanged in reply, but that was all.

Crabb stealthily arose and peered into the lighted window. It was a study. The light came from a lamp with a green shade. Under its glow upon the desk were maps and documents in profusion. And in the corner he could make out the lines of an iron-bound chest or box. They had made no mistake. Unless in the possession of Von Schlichter it was here that the Chinese treaty would be found.

"All right," whispered Crabb. "An old-fashioned padlock, too."

Crabb tried the window. It was locked. He took something from one of the pockets of his coat and reached up to the middle of the sash. There was a sound like the quick shearing of linen which sent the blood back to Burnett's heart. In the still night it seemed to come back manifold from the wings of the buildings opposite. They paused again. A slight crackling of broken glass, and Crabb's long fingers reached through the hole and turned the catch. In a moment they were in the room.

The intangible and Quixotic had become a latter-day reality. Burnett's spirits rose. He did not lack courage, and here was a situation which spurred him to the utmost.

Instinctively he closed the inside shutters behind him. From the alley the pair would not have presented an appearance which accorded with the quiet splendor of the room. He found himself peering around, his ears straining for the slightest sound.

A glance revealed the dispatch-box, heavy, squat and phlegmatic, like its owner. Crabb had tiptoed over to the door of the adjoining room. Burnett saw the eyes dilate and the warning finger to his lips.

From the inner apartment, slowly and regularly, came the sound of heavy breathing. There, in a broad armchair by the foot of the bed, sprawled the baron's valet, in stertorous sleep. His mouth was wide open, his limbs relaxed. He had heard nothing.

"Quick," whispered Crabb; "your bandanna around his legs."

Burnett surprised himself by the rapidity and intelligence of his collaboration. A handkerchief was slipped into the man's mouth, and before his eyes were fairly opened he was gagged and bound hand and foot by the cord from the baron's own dressing gown.

From a pocket Crabb had produced a revolver, which he flourished significantly under the nose of the terrified man, who recoiled before the dark look which accompanied it.

Crabb seemed to have planned exactly what to do. He took a bath towel and tied it over the man's ears and under his chin. From the bed he took the baron's sheets and blankets, enswathing the unfortunate servant until nothing but the tip of his nose was visible. A rope of suspenders and cravats completed the job.

The Baron Arnim's valet, to all the purposes of usefulness in life, was a bundled mummy.

"*Phew!*" said Crabb, when it was done. "*Poor devil!* But it can't be helped. He mustn't see or know. And now for it."

Crabb produced a bunch of skeleton keys and an electric bull's-eye. He tried the keys rapidly. In a moment the dispatch-box was opened and its contents exposed to view.

"Carefully now," whispered Crabb. "What should it look like?"

"A foolscap-shaped thing in silk covers with dangling cords," said Ross. "There, under your hand."

In a moment they had it out and between them on the desk. There it was, in all truth, written in two columns, Chinese on the one side, French on the other.

"Are you sure?" said Crabb.

"Sure! Sure as I'm a thief in the night!"

"Then sit and write, man. Write as you never wrote before. I'll listen and watch Rameses the Second."

In the twenty minutes during which Burnett fearfully wrote, Crabb stood listening at the doors and windows for sounds of servants or approaching carriages. The man swaddled in the sheets made a few futile struggles and then subsided. Burnett's eyes gleamed. Other eyes than his would gleam at what he saw and wrote. When he finished he closed the document, removed all traces of his work, replaced it in the iron box and shut the lid. He dropped the precious sheets into an inner pocket and was moving toward the window when Crabb seized him by the arm. There was a step in the hallway without, and the door opened. There, stout and grizzled, his walrus mustache bristling with surprise, in all the distinction of gold lace and orders, stood Baron Arnim.

CHAPTER V

FOR a moment there was no sound. The burglars looked at the Baron and the Baron looked at the burglars, mouths and eyes open alike. Then, even before Crabb could display his intimidating revolver, the German had disappeared through the door screaming at the top of his lungs.

"Quick! Out of the window!" said Crabb, helping Burnett over the sill. "Down you go—I'll follow. Don't fall. If you miss your footing, we're ruined."

Burnett scrambled out, over the coping and down the ladder, Crabb almost on his fingers. But they reached the yard in safety and were out in the alley running in the shadow of the fence before a venturesome head stuck forth from the open window and a revolver blazed into the vacant air.

"The devil!" said Crabb. "They'll have

every copper in the city on us in a minute. *This way.*" He turned into a narrow alley at right angles to the other. "Off with the coat as you go—now, the mustache and grease paint. *Take* your time. Into this sewer with the coats. So!"

Two gentlemen in light topcoats, one in a cap, the other in a hat, walked up *N* street arm in arm, thickly singing. *Their* shirt fronts and hair were rumpled, their legs were not too steady, and they clung affectionately to each other for support and sang thickly.

A window flew up and a tousled head appeared.

"Hey!" yelled a voice. "Burglars in the alley!"

"Burglars!" said one of the singers; and then: "Go to bed. You're drunk."

More sounds of windows, the blowing of night whistles and hurrying feet.

Still the revelers sang on.

A stout policeman, clamorous and bellicose, broke in.

"Did you see 'em? Did you see 'em?" he cried, glaring into their faces. Bleary eyes returned his look.

"W-who?" said the voices in unison.

"Burglars," roared the copper. "If I wasn't busy I'd run ye in." And he was off at full speed on his vagrant mission.

"Lucky you're busy, old chap," muttered Crabb to the departing figure. "Do sober up a little, Ross, or we'll never get away. And don't jostle me so, for I clank like a bell-wether."

Slowly the pair made their way to *T*homas Circle and Vermont Avenue, where the sounds of commotion were lost in the noises of the night.

At L Street Burnett straightened up. "Lord!" he gasped. "But that was close."

"Not as close as it looked," said Crabb, coolly. "A white shirt-front does wonders with a copper. It was better than a knock on the head and a run for it. In the meanwhile, Ross, for the love of Heaven, help me with some of the bric-à-brac." And with that he handed Burnett a gold pin tray, a silver box and a watch fob.

Burnett soberly examined the spoils. "I only wish we could have done without that."

"And had Arnim know what we were driving for? Never, Ross. I'll pawn them in New York for as little as I can and send von Schlichter the tickets. Won't that do?"

"I suppose it must," said Burnett, dubiously.

By three o'clock they were on the *Blue Wing* again, Burnett with mingled feelings of doubt and satisfaction, Crabb afire with the achievement.

"Rasselas was a fool, Ross, a malcontent—a *fainéant*. Life is amazing, bewitching, consummate." And then, gayly: "Here's a health, boy—a long life to the new ambassador to the Court of St. James!"

But Ross did not go to the Court of St.

James. In the following winter, to the surprise of many, the *P*resident gave him a special mission to prepare a trade treaty with
*P*eru. Baron Arnim, in due course, recovered
his bric-à-brac. Meanwhile Emperor William, mystified at the amazing sagacity of the
Secretary of State in the Eastern question,
continues the building of a mighty navy in the
fear that one day the upstart nation across the
ocean will bring the questions complicating
them to an issue.

But life was no longer amusing, bewitching or consummate to Crabb. The flavor of
an adventure gone from his mouth, the com-
monplace became more flat and tasteless than
before. Life was all pale drabs and grays
again. To make matters worse he had been
obliged to make a business visit in Philadelphia, and this filled the cup of insipidity to
the brim. He was almost ready to wish that
his benighted forbears had never owned the
coal mines in *P*ennsylvania to which he had
fallen heir, for it seemed there were many

matters to be settled, contracts to be signed
and leases to be drawn by his attorney in the
sleepy city, and it would be several days, he
discovered, before he could get off to *New-
port*. *N*ot even the *Blue Wing* was at his
disposal, for an accident in the engine room
had laid her out of commission for two weeks
at least.

So he resigned himself to the inevitable, and
took a room at a hotel, grimly determined to
see the matter through, conscious meanwhile
of a fervid hope that the unusual might happen—the lightning might strike. Hate he had
known and fear, but love had so far eluded
him. Why, he did not know, save that he
had never been willing to perceive that emotion when offered in conventional forms—and
since no other forms were possible, he had
simply ceased to consider the matter. Yet
marry some day, he must, of course. But
whom? Little he dreamed how soon he would
know. Little did Miss *Patricia* Wharton
think that she had anything to do with it.

In fact, *Patricia's* thoughts at that time were far from matrimony. *Patricia* was bored. For à month while Wharton père boiled out his gout at the sulphur springs, *Patricia* had dutifully sat and rocked, tapping a small foot impatiently, looking hourly less a monument of *Patience* and smiling not at all.

At last they were in *Philadelphia*. Wilson had opened two rooms at the house and a speedy termination of David Wharton's business would have seen them soon at Bar Harbor. But something went wrong at the office in Chestnut Street, and *Patricia*, once a lamb and now a sheep of sacrifice, found herself at this particular moment doomed to another weary week of waiting.

To make matters worse not a girl *Patricia* knew was in town, or if there were any the telephone refused to discover them. Her aunt's place was at Haverford, but she knew that an invitation to dinner there meant aged Quaker cousins and that kind of creaky informality which shows a need of oil at the

joints. *T*hat lubricant *P*atricia had no in-
tention of supplying. She had rather be bored
alone than bored in company. She found herself sighing for Bar Harbor as she had never
sighed before. She pictured the cottage, cool
and gray among the rocks, the blue bowl of
the sea with its rim just at her window-ledge,
the clamoring surf, and the briny smell with
its faint suggestion of things cool and curious
which came up newly breathed from the heart
of the deep. She could hear "Country Girl"
whinnying impatience from the stable when
Jack Masters on "Kentucky" rode down from
"The *P*innacle" to inquire.

Indeed, as she walked out into the Square
in the afternoon she found herself relapsing
into a minute and somewhat sordid introspec-
tion. It was the weather, perhaps. Surely the
dog-days had settled upon the sleepy city in
earnest. *N*o breath stirred the famishing
trees, the smell of hot asphalt was in the air,
locusts buzzed vigorously everywhere, trolley
bells clanged out of tune, and the sun was

leaving a blood-hot trail across the sky in angry augury for the morrow.

Patricia sank upon a bench, and poked viciously at the walk with her parasol. She experienced a certain grim satisfaction in being more than usually alone. *Poor Patricia!* who at the crooking of a finger, could have summoned to her side any one of five estimable scions of stupid, distinguished families. Only something new, something difficult and extraordinary would lift her from the hopeless slough of despond into which she had found herself precipitated.

Andromeda awaiting *Perseus* on a bench in Rittenhouse Square! She smiled widely and unrestrainedly up and precisely into the face of Mr. Mortimer Crabb.

CHAPTER VI

A PLEASANT face it was, upon which, to her surprise, a smile very suddenly grew into being as though in response to her own. Patricia's eyes dropped quickly—sedately, as became those of a decorous woman, and yet in that brief second in which the eyes of the tall young man met hers, she had noticed that they were gray, as though sun-bleached, but very clear and sparkling. And when she raised her own to look quite through and beyond the opposite bench, her conscience refused to deny that she had enjoyed the looking. Were the eyes smiling *at,* or *with* her? In that distinction lay a question in morals. Was their sparkle quizzical or intrusive? She would have vowed that good humor, benevolence (if benevolence may be found in the eyes of two and thirty), and a certain polite interest were

its actual ingredients. It was all very interesting. She surprised herself in a not un-
lively curiosity as to his life and calling, and
in a lack of any sort of misgiving at the *con-
tretemps.*

The shadows beneath the wilted trees grew
deeper. The sun swept down into the west
and suddenly vanished with all his train of
gold and purple. *Patricia* stole a furtive look
at her neighbor. *T*riumphantly she confirmed
her diagnosis. The man was lost in the glow
of the sunset. Importunity and he were miles
asunder.

It may have been that *Patricia's* eyes were
more potent than the sunset, or that her
triumphant deduction was based upon a false
premise, or that the young man had been
watching her all the while from the tail of his
benevolent eye; for without the slightest
warning, his head turned suddenly to find the
eyes of the unfortunate *Patricia* again fixed
upon his. However quickly she might turn
aside, the glance exchanged was long enough

to disclose the fact that the sparkle was still there and to excite a suspicion that it had never been dispelled. Nor did the character of the smile reassure her. She was not at all certain now that he was not smiling both *with* and *at* her.

The quickly averted head, the toss of the chin, seemed all too inadequate to the situation; yet she availed herself of those bulwarks of maiden modesty in virtuous effort to refute the unconscious testimony of her unlucky eyes. Instinct suggested immediate flight. But Patricia moved not. Here indeed was a case where flight meant confession. She felt rather than saw his gaze search her from head to foot, and struggle as she might against it, the warm color raced to her cheek and brow. If she had enjoyed the situation a moment before, the impertinence, so suddenly born, filled her with dismay. By some subtle feminine process of reasoning, she succeeded in eliminating her share in the trifling adventure and now saw only the sin of the offending male.

At last she arose the very presentment of injured and scornful dignity and walked, looking neither to the left hand nor to the right.

There was a sound of firm, rapid footsteps
and then a deep voice at her elbow.

"I beg pardon," it was saying.

The lifted straw hat, the inclined head, the
mellow tones, the gray eyes (again benevolent), however unalarming in themselves,
filled her with very real inquietude. Whatever he had done before, this, surely, was in-
supportable. She was about to turn away
when her eye fell upon his extended arm and
upon her luckless parasol.

"I beg pardon," he repeated, "but isn't this
yours?"

The blood flew to her face again and it was
with an embarrassment, a *gaucherie,* the like
of which she could not remember, that she extended her hand toward the errant sunshade.
No sound came from her lips; with bent head
she took it from him. But as she walked on,
she found that he was walking, too—with her,

" 'I beg pardon,' he repeated, 'but isn't this yours?' "

directly at her side. For a moment she was cold with terror.

"I hope you'll let me go along," he was saying coolly, "I'm really quite harmless. If you knew—if you only knew how dreadfully bored I've been, you really wouldn't mind me at all."

Patricia stole a hurried glance at him, her fears curiously diminished.

"I'm what the fallen call a victim of circumstances," he went on. "I ask no worse fate for my dearest enemy than to be consigned without a friend to this wilderness of whitened stoops and boarded doors—to wait upon your city's demigod, Procrastination. This I've done for forty-eight hours with a dear memory of a past but without a hope for the future. If the Fountain of Youth were to gush hopefully from the office water-cooler of my aged lawyer, he would eye it askance and sigh for the lees of the turbid Schuykill."

However she strove to lift her brows, Patricia was smiling now in spite of herself.

"I've followed the meandering tide down the narrow cañon you call Chestnut Street, watched the leisurely coal wagon and its attendant tail of trolleys, or sat in my hotel striving to dust aside the accumulating cobwebs, one small unquiet molecule of disconsolation. I'm stranded—marooned. By comparison, Crusoe was gregarious."

During this while they were walking north. All the way to Chestnut Street, Patricia was wondering whether to be most alarmed or amused. Of one thing she was assured, she was bored no longer. A sense of the violence done to her traditions hung like a millstone around her neck; and yet *Patricia* found herself peeping avidly through the hole to listen to the seductive voice of unconvention.

When *Patricia* succeeded in summoning her voice, she was not quite sure that it was her own.

"You're an impertinent person," she found herself saying.

"Can't you forgive?"

"*No.*"

"Circumstances are against me," he said, "but I give you my word, I've a place in my own city, a friend or two, and a certain proclivity for virtue."

"Even if you do—speak to strange——"

"But I don't. It was the blessed parasol. Otherwise I shouldn't have dared."

"And the proclivity for virtue——"

"Why, that's exactly the reason. Can't you see? It was you! You fairly exuded gentility. Come now, I'm humility itself. I've sinned. How can I expiate?"

"By letting me go home to dinner."

Patricia was laughing this time. The man was looking at his watch.

"What a brute I am!" He stopped, took off his hat and turned away. And here it was that some little frivolous genius put unmeditated words upon *Patricia's* tongue.

"I'm not so dreadfully hungry," she said.

After all, he had been impertinent so very courteously.

In a moment he was at her side again.

"That was kind of you. Perhaps you've forgiven me."

"N—no," with rising inflection.

"Come now! Let's be friends, just for this little while. Let's begin at once to believe we've known each other always—just for to-night. I will be getting out of town to-morrow and we won't meet again. I'm certain of that."

"How can I be sure?" Patricia spoke as though thinking aloud.

"They've promised me this time. I'll go away to-morrow. If my papers aren't ready I'll leave without them."

"Will you give me your word?"

"Upon my honor."

Patricia turned for the first time and looked directly up at him. What value could she set upon the honor of one she knew not?

Whatever the feminine process of examination, she seemed satisfied.

"What can I do? It's almost dusk."

"I was about to suggest—er—I thought perhaps you might be willing to—er—go and have a bite—to eat—in fact, dinner."

Patricia stopped and looked up at him in startled abstraction. The word and its train of associated ideas evolved in significant fashion from her mental topsy-turvy. Dinner! With a strange man in a public place! The prosaic word took new and curious meanings unwritten upon the lexicon of her code. *There* was the tangible presentation of her sin—that she might read and run while there was yet time. How had it all happened? What had this insolent person said to make it possible for her to forget herself for so long?

With no word of explanation her small feet went hurrying down the hill while his big ones strode protestingly alongside.

"Well?" he said at last.

But she gave him no answer and only walked the faster.

"You're going?"

"Home—at once." She spoke with cold incisiveness.

He walked along a few moments in silence —then said assertively:

"You're afraid."

For reply she only shook her head.

"It's true," he went on. "You're afraid. A moment ago, you were willing to forget we had just met. Now in a breath you're willing to forget that we've met at all."

But she would not answer.

He glanced at the poise of the haughty head just below his own. Was it mock virtue? He felt thoroughly justified in believing it so.

They had reached a corner. Patricia stopped.

"You'll let me go here, won't you? You'll not follow me or try to find out anything, will you? Say you won't, please, please! It has all been a dreadful mistake—how dreadful I didn't know until—until just now. I must go—alone, you understand—alone——"

"But it is getting dark, you——"

"*No*, no! It doesn't matter. I'm not afraid. How can I be—now? *P*lease let me go—alone. Good-by!"

And in a moment she had vanished in the cross street.

CHAPTER VII

MORTIMER CRABB watched the retreating figure.

"H-m," he said, "the Eternal Question—as usual—without the answer. And yet I would have sworn that that parasol in the Square——"

He had always possessed an attitude of amused and tolerant patronage for the City of Brotherly Love—it was the birthright of any typical *N*ew Yorker—and yet since that inconsiderable adventure in Rittenhouse Square, he had discovered undreamed-of virtues in the *P*ennsylvania metropolis. It was a city not of apartments, but of homes—homes in which men lived with their families and brought up interesting children in the old-fashioned way—a city of conservative progress, of historic association, of well-guarded tradition—an American city, in short—which

74

New York was not. At the Bachelors' Club he sang its praises, and mentioned a plan of wintering there, but was laughed at for his pains. Anything unusual and extraordinary was to be expected of Mortimer Crabb. But a winter in *Philadelphia! T*his was too preposterous.

Crabb said nothing in reply. He only smiled politely and when the *Blue Wing* was put in commission went off on a cruise with no other company but his thoughts and Captain Jepson. Jepson under ordinary circumstances would have been sufficient, but now Mortimer Crabb spent much time in a deck chair reading in a book of poems, or idly gazing at the swirl of foam in the vessel's wake. Jepson wondered what he was thinking of, for Crabb was not a man to spend much time in dreaming, and the Captain would have given much that he possessed to know. He would have been surprised if Mortimer Crabb had told him. To tell the truth Crabb was thinking—of a parasol. He was wondering if after all, his judgment had been erring. The lady in the Square had left the parasol, it was true. But then all the tribe of parasols and umbrellas seemed born to the fate of being neglected and forgotten, and there was no reason why this particular specimen of the genus should be exempt from the frailties of its kind. As he remembered, it was a flimsy thing of green silk and lace, obviously a French frippery which might be readily guilty of such a form of naughtiness.

It had long worried him to think that he might have misjudged the sleeping princess— as he had learned to call her—and he knew that it would continue to worry him until he proved the matter one way or another for himself. Had she really forgotten the parasol? Or had she—not forgotten it?

The cruise ended, the summer lengthened into fall, and winter found Mortimer Crabb established in residence at a fashionable hotel in *P*hiladelphia.

Letters had come from *N*ew York to cer-

tain *Philadelphia* dowagers in the councils of
the mighty, to the end that in due course
Crabb accepted for several desirable dinners,
and before he knew he found himself in the
full swing of a social season. And so when
the night of the Assembly came around, he
found himself dining at the house of one of
his sponsors in a party wholly given over to
the magnification of three tremulous young fe-
male persons, who were to receive their *cachet*
and certificate of eligibility in attending that
ancient and honorable function.

It was just at the top of the steps leading
to the foyer of the ball-room that Crabb met
Patricia Wharton in the crowd, face to face.
The encounter was unavoidable. He saw
the brief question in her glance before she
placed him, the vanishing smile, the momentary pallor, and then was conscious that she
had gone by, her eyes looking past him, her
brows slightly raised, her lips drawn together,
the very letter of indifference and contempt.
It was cutting advanced to the dignity of a

fine art. Crabb felt the color rise to his temples and heard the young bud at his side saying:

"What is it, Mr. Crabb? You look as if you'd seen the ghost of all your past transgressions."

"*All* of them, Miss Cheston! Oh, I hope I don't look as bad as that," he laughed. "Only one—a very tiny one."

"Do tell me," cried the bud.

"First, let's safely run the gantlet of the lorgnons."

When the party was assembled and past the grenadiers who jealously guard the sacred inner bulwarks, Crabb was glad to relinquish his companion to another, while he sought seclusion behind a bank of azaleas to watch the moving dancers. So she really *was* somebody. He began, for a moment, to doubt the testimony of the vagrant glances and the guilty parasol. Could he have been mistaken? Had she really forgotten the parasol after all? The situation was brutal enough for her and he was quite prepared to respect her delicacy. What he did resent was the way in which she had done it. She had taken to cover angrily and stood at bay with all her woman's weapons sharpened. The curl of lip and narrowed eye bespoke a degree of disdain quite out of proportion to the offense. But he made a rapid resolution not to seek her or meet her eye. If his was the fault, it was the only reparation he could offer her.

As he whirled around the room with his little bud, he caught a glimpse of her upon the opposite side and so maneuvered that he would come no nearer. When he had guided his partner to a seat, it did not take him long to gratify a very natural curiosity.

"Will you tell me," he asked, "who—no, don't look now—the girl in the black spangly dress is?"

"Who? Where?" asked Miss Cheston. "*Patricia?* you mean? Of course! Miss Wharton, my cousin. Haven't you met her?"

"Er—no! She's good-looking."

"Isn't she? And the dearest creature—but rather cold and the least bit prim."

"Pri—Oh, really!"

"Yes! We're Quakers, you know. She belongs to the older set. *Perhaps* that's why she seems a trifle cold and—er—conventional."

"Convent—! Oh, yes, of course."

"You know we're really quite a breezy lot, if you only know us. Some of this year's debs are really very dreadful."

"How shocking, and Miss Wharton is not dreadful?"

"Oh, dear, no. But she is awfully good fun. Come, you must meet her. Let me take you over."

But good fortune in the person of Stephen Ventnor intervened.

It was the unexpected which was to happen. Crabb was returning from the table with a favor. His eye ran along the line of chairs in a brief fruitless search. Mr. Barclay, who was leading the cotillion, caught his eye at this precise psychological moment.

"Stranded, Crabb? Let me present you to——"

He mentioned no name but was off in a moment winding in and out among those on the floor. Crabb followed. When he had succeeded in eluding the imminent dancers and had reached the other side of the room, there was Barclay bending over.

"Awfully nice chap—stranger," he was saying, and then aloud, "Miss Wharton, may I present—Mr. Crabb?"

It was all over in a moment. The crowded room had hidden the black dress and the fair hair. But it was too late. Barclay was off in a second and there they were looking again into each other's eyes, *Patricia* pale and cold as stone, Crabb a trifle ill at ease at the awkward situation which, however appearances were against him, was none of his choosing.

Crabb inclined his head and extended the hand which carried his favor. They both glanced down, seeking in that innocent trinket a momentary refuge from the predicament.

81

It was then for the first time that Crabb discovered the thing he was offering her—a little frivolous green silk parasol.

She looked up at him again, her eyes blazing, but she rose to her feet and looked around her as though seeking some mode of escape. He fully expected that she would refuse to dance, and was preparing to withdraw as gracefully as he might when, with chin erect and eyes which looked and carried her spirit quite beyond him, she took the parasol and followed him upon the floor.

But the subtlety of suggestion which seemed to possess Crabb's particular little comedy was to be still more amusingly developed. The figure in which they became a part was a pretty vari-colored whirl of flowers and ribbons, in which the green parasols were destined to play a part. For a miniature Maypole was brought and the parasols were fastened to the depending ribbons in accordance with their color.

As the figure progressed and the dancers

interwove, Crabb could not fail to note the recurrent intentional snub. He felt himself blameless in the unlucky situation, and this needless display of hostility so clearly expressed seemed made in very bad taste. Each time he passed the flaunted shoulder, the upcast chin, or curling lip, he found his humility to be growing less and less until as the dance neared its end he glowed with a very righteous ire. If she had meant to deny him completely, she should have chosen the opportunity when he had first come up. And as he passed her, he rejoiced in the discovery that she had inadvertently chosen the other end of the ribbon attached to the very parasol which he bore. When the May dance was over, Miss Wharton found Mr. Crabb at her side handing her the green parasol precisely as he had handed her that other one in the Square six months before.

"I beg pardon," he was saying quizzically, "but isn't this yours?"

The accent and benevolent eye were unmistakable. If there were any arrow in her quiver of scorn unshot, his effrontery completely disarmed her. If looks could have killed, Crabb must have died at once. Assured of the depths of his infamy, she could only murmur rather faintly:

"I shall go to my seat, at once, please." Indeed, Crabb was a very lively corpse. He was smiling coolly down at her.

"Certainly, if you wish it. Only—er—I hope you'll let me go along."

How she hated him! The words uttered again with the same smiling effrontery seemed to be burned anew into her memory. Could she never be free from this inevitable man? Her seat was at the far end of the room.

"I think you have done me some injustice," he said quietly, and then, "It has been a pleasant dance. Thank you so much."

"*Thank you,*" replied *Patricia* acidly, and he was gone.

CHAPTER VIII

MISS WHARTON rather crossly dismissed her weary maid, and threw herself into an armchair. Odious situation! Her peccadillo had found her out! What made the matter still worse was the ingenuous impeccability of her villain. On every hand she heard his praises sung. And it vexed her that she had been unable to contribute anything to his detriment. Of course, after seeing her leave the parasol it would have been stupid of him to—to let her forget it. In her thoughts that adventure had long since been condoned. It was this new *rencontre* which had so upset her. It angered her to think how little delicacy he gave her credit for when he had asked Jack Barclay to present him. If they had met by chance, it would have been different. She would have been sharply civil, but not retrospective; and would have trusted to his sense of the situation to be the same. *T*hat he had assailed her helpless barriers, wrote him down a brute, divested him of all the garments of sensibility in which she had clothed him. It angered her to think that her fancy had seen fit to make him any other than he was. But mingled with her anger, she was surprised to discover disappointment, too. It was this—this person who shared with her the secret of her one iniquity.

She pulled impatiently at her long gloves and arose with an air of finality. And so Miss Wharton put the importunate Mr. Crabb entirely from her mind; until the following *T*hursday night at the dinner at the Hollingsworths'.

"*Patty*, dear, have you met Mr. Crabb?" Mrs. Hollingsworth was saying.

Miss Wharton had, at the Assembly.

Mr. Crabb politely echoed; and *Patricia* hated him for the nebulous smile which seemed to contain hidden meanings. But she rose to the occasion in a way which seemed to disconcert her companion—who only answered her rapid fire of commonplaces in monosyllables. At the table she found her refuge upon the other side to be an Italian from the embassy at Washington, whose French limped but whose English was a cripple. And so they minced and stuttered, Ollendorf fashion, through the oysters and soup, while Crabb occupied himself with the daughter of the house upon his other side. But at last *Patty* was aware that Mr. Crabb was speaking.

"Miss Wharton," he began, "I fear I've been put somewhat under a cloud."

"Really," she answered sweetly, "how so?"

A little disconcerted but undismayed, he continued:

"Because of the manner of our meeting."

"Our meeting!" she said uncertainly.

"At the Assembly, you know. I thought perhaps that—you thought—I'd asked to be presented."

"Didn't you? *Then*, how did we happen to meet?"

He could not but admire her *sang-froid*. She was smiling a non-committal smile at the centerpiece.

"Er—I should explain. I was adrift and Barclay came to my rescue. I give you my word, I had no notion it was to you he was taking me. It was all over in a second."

"*Then* you really didn't wish to meet me? I'm so sorry."

She had turned her face slowly to his and was looking him levelly in the eyes. It was a challenge, not a petition. He met her thrust fairly.

"My dear Miss Wharton," he smiled, "how could I know what you were like—er —if I'd never seen you?"

*T*his time he fairly set her weapon flying.

"What I wish you to understand," he continued, steadily, "is that I didn't know that Barclay was taking me to you. I wish credit

88

for a certain delicacy. I should not have cared to force myself upon you."

"I'm sure I shouldn't have minded in the least," she said, lightly. "I'm not so difficult as all that."

As soon as she had spoken she knew she had overshot her mark.

"That's awfully good of you, you know. I'm sure you'll admit I had no means of knowing," he added, "how difficult you were."

She flushed a little before returning to the attack.

"Of course a girl wishes to know a little something about a man before——"

"Before she permits herself to misjudge him." He smiled. "Candidly, do you feel in any better position to judge me now than you did before——"

"Before the Assembly?" she interrupted. "I think so. You don't eat with your knife," laughing. "You've a respect for the napkin. People say you're clever. Why shouldn't I believe them?"

89

"If this is your creed of morality, I'm respectability itself. Can you doubt me? Why won't you be frank? If I'm respectable why shouldn't you have cared to meet me?"

"I'm not sure I thought very much about it. How did you know I didn't wish to meet you?"

"How could I know you did?"

She looked up at him, a new expression on her face.

"I didn't," she said quietly, "I—I—abhorred the very thought of you."

Crabb looked contemplatively at his truffle. "I thank you for your candor," he replied at last.

*T*hen after a pause, "If you'll forgive me, I'll promise not to mention the subject again."

"And if I don't forgive you?"

"You're at my mercy for this hour at least," he laughed.

"I can still fly to Italy," she replied. "I could forgive you, I think, but for one thing."

He looked the question.

"*T*his dinner. Is it to chance that I'm indebted for the—the—honor of your society?"

Crabb's gaze had dropped to the table, but she had seen just such a sparkle in them once before. Nor when he looked at her had it disappeared.

"You mean——"

She continued gazing at him steadily.

"You mean—did I arrange it?" he asked.

*P*atricia bowed her head.

"How could I have done so?" he urged.

"Isn't *N*ick Hollingsworth an intimate friend of yours?"

"Yes, but I fail to see——"

"Will you deny it?"

"I'm afraid you'll have to take me a little on faith," he pleaded. "At any rate you will not suffer long. I'm leaving town in a few days."

"For long?" she asked politely.

"For good, I think. Won't you let me come in to see you before then?"

"*P*erhaps——"

But Mrs. Hollingsworth had cast her glance down the line and drawn back her chair.

When the men came down into the drawing room, Mr. Crabb discovered that Miss Wharton had carefully ensconced herself in the center of a perimeter of skirts, which defied disintegration and apportionment. There was music and afterwards a call for carriages. So Mr. Crabb saw no more of Miss Wharton upon that night. Nor, indeed, did *Patricia* see him again. The following day he called. She was out. Then came a note and some roses. Business had called him sooner than he had expected. He begged to assure her of his distinguished consideration; would she forgive him now that he was gone, accept this new impertinence and forget all those that had gone before?

Patricia accepted the impertinence; and for many days it filled her little white room with seductive odors that made his last admonition more difficult.

CHAPTER IX

THE months of winter passed and Crabb returned not. July found the Whartons again at Bar Harbor. Patricia would go out for hours in her canoe or her sailboat, rejoicing with bronzed cheek and hardening muscles in the buffets and caresses of Frenchman's Bay. It was a very tiny catboat that she had learned to manage herself and in which she would tolerate no male hand at the helm except in the stiffest blows.

One quiet afternoon, early in August, she was sailing alone down toward Sorrento. It was one of those brilliant New England days when every detail of water and sky shone clear as an amethyst. Here and there a sail cut a sharp yellow rhomboid from the velvet woods. Patricia listened idly to the lapping of the tiny waves and found herself thinking again rather uncomfortably of the one person who had caught her off her guard and kept her there. If he had only stayed in Philadelphia one week more, she could at least have retired with drums beating and colors flying.

A sound distracted her. She looked to leeward under the lifting sail and on her bow, well out in the open off Stave Island, she could make out the lines of an overturned canoe and two figures in the water. She quickly loosed the sheet and shifted her helm and bore down rapidly upon the unfortunates. She could see a man bearing upon one end of the canoe lifting the other into the air, trying to get the water out; but each time he did so, a bull terrier dog swam to the gunwale and overturned it again. She sped by to leeward and, skilfully turning her little craft upon its heel, came up into the wind alongside.

"How do you do?" said the moistful person, smiling.

The hair was streaked down into his eyes. He hardly wondered that she didn't recognize him.

"Mr. Crabb!" she said at last, rather faintly, "how did you happen——"

"It was the dog," he said cheerfully. "I thought he understood canoes."

"He might have drowned you. Why, it's Jack Masters' '*T*eddy,'" she cried. "Here, *T*eddy, come aboard at once, sir." She bent over the low freeboard and by dint of much hauling managed to get him in.

In the meantime, the catboat had drifted away from the canoe. Crabb had at last succeeded in getting in and was now bailing with his cap.

"Won't you come over?" shouted *P*atricia.

"Oh, I'm all right," he returned. "It was the dog I was worried about." Then for the first time he was aware that the paddle had drifted off and was now floating a hundred yards away.

"I'm sorry, but my paddle is adrift."

So *P*atricia, amid much barking from the rejuvenated *T*eddy, came alongside again.

*T*here sat the bedraggled and dripping

Crabb in three inches of water, his empty hands upon the gunwales, looking rather foolishly up at the blue eyes that were smiling rather whimsically down.

She could not resist the temptation to banter him. Had she prayed for vengeance, nothing could have been sent to her sweeter than this.

"You look rather—er—glum," she said.

"I'm not," he replied, calmly. "I've not been so happy in months."

"What on earth is there to prevent my sailing off and leaving you?" she laughed.

"*Nothing*," he said. "I'm all right. I'll swim for the paddle when I'm rested."

"Have you thought I might take that with me, too?" she asked sweetly.

"All right," he laughed, trying to suppress the chattering teeth. "Somebody'll be along presently."

"Don't be too sure. You're really very much at my mercy."

"You were not always so unkind."

"Mr. Crabb!" *Patricia* retired in confusion to the tiller. "You're impudent!" She hauled in her sheet and the boat gathered headway.

"*Please,* Miss Whárton, please!" he shouted. But *Patricia* did not move from the tiller, and the catboat glided off. He watched her sail down and recover the paddle and then head back toward him.

"Won't you forgive me and take me in?"

"I suppose I must. But I'm sure I'd rather you'd drown. I'm hardly in the mood for coals of fire."

"I am, though," he chattered, "for I'm d—deucedly c—cold."

"You don't deserve it. But if you were drowned I suppose I'd be to blame. I wouldn't have you on my conscience again for anything."

"*T*hen please take me on your boat."

"Will you behave yourself?"

"I'll try."

"And never again refer to—to——"

"Um——"

"*T*hen please come in—out of the wet."

It was toward the end of August when the southeast wind had raised a gray and thunderous sea, that two persons sat under the lee of a rock near Great Head and watched the giant breakers shatter themselves to foam. *T*hey sat very close together, and the little they said was drowned in the roar of the elements. But they did not care. *T*hey were willing just to sit and watch the fruitless struggles of the swollen waters.

"Won't you tell me," said the girl at last, "about that dinner? Didn't you really ask Mrs. Hollingsworth to send you in with me?"

The man looked amusedly off at the jagged horizon.

"No, I really didn't," he said, and then, after a pause, with a laugh: "but *N*ick did."

"Whited sepulcher!" said the girl. Another pause. *T*his time the man questioned:

"*T*here is another thing—won't you tell

me? About the parasol last summer—did you forget it, really—or—or—just leave it?"

"Mortimer!" she cried, flushing furiously. "I didn't!"

But he assisted her in hiding her face, smiling down benevolently the while.

"Really? Honestly? *T*ruly?" he said, softly.

"I didn't—I didn't," she repeated.

"Didn't what?" he still persevered.

She looked up at him for a moment, flushed more furiously than before and sought refuge anew. But the muffled reply was perfectly distinguishable to the man.

"I—I—*didn't*—forget it."

But the Great Head rocks didn't hear.

*T*hus Mortimer Crabb, having spent much of his time in making opportunities for other people, had at last succeeded in making one for himself.

He had the pleasure of knowing, too, that he was also making one for *P*atty—not that this was Miss Wharton's first opportunity,

99

for everyone knew that her rather sedate demeanor concealed a capricious coquetry which she could no more control than she could the music of the spheres. But this was going to be a different kind of opportunity, for Crabb had decided that not only was she going to be engaged to him, but that when the time came she was going to marry him.

*T*his decision reached, he spent all of his time in convincing her that he was the one man in the world exactly suited to her protean moods. The sum of his possessions had not been made known to her, and he delighted in planning his surprise. So that when the *Blue Wing* appeared in the harbor, he invited her for a sail in her own catboat, calmly took the helm in spite of her protests, and before she was aware of it, had made a neat landing at his own gangway. Jepson poked his head over the side and welcomed them, grinning broadly, and, following Crabb's inviting gesture, *Patricia* went up on deck feeling very much like the lady who had married the Lord of Burleigh. Then Jepson gave some mysterious orders and before long she was reclining luxuriously in a deck chair and the *Blue Wing* was breasting the surges which showed the way to the open sea.

" 'All of this,' " quoted Crabb gayly, with a fine gesture which comprehended the whole of the North Atlantic Ocean, " 'is mine and thine.' "

"It's very nice of you to be so rich. Why didn't you tell me?" said Patricia.

"Because I had a certain pride in wanting you to like me for myself."

"You think I would have married you for your money?"

"Oh, yes," he said, promptly, "of course you would. A rich man has about as much chance of entering the Kingdom of Romance as the Biblical camel has to get through the eye of the needle."

"Why is it then that I find you so very much more attractive now that I've found the *Blue Wing?*"

"But you found *me* first," he laughed.

"Did I?" archly.

"If you still doubt it, there's the parasol!"

The mention of the parasol always silenced her.

CHAPTER X

THAT was one of many cruises, and the *Blue Wing* contributed not a little to the gayety of the waning days of summer at Mount Desert. It was the *Blue Wing,* too, that in early September brought the Wharton family, bag and baggage, southward to Philadelphia, where Mortimer Crabb lingered, hoping to exact a promise of marriage before Christmas. But Patricia would make no promises. She had a will of her own, her fiancé discovered, and had no humor to forego the independence of her spinsterhood for the responsibilities which awaited her. It was in this situation that Crabb discovered himself to be possessed of surprising virtues in tolerance and tact. Patricia, he knew, had many admirers. The woods at Bar Harbor had been, both figuratively and literally, filled with them, and most of them had been eligible. Jack Masters, and Stephen Ventnor, who lived in *Philadelphia*, were still warm in pursuit of the fair quarry, who had not yet consented to an announcement of her engagement to Crabb.

But these men caused him little anxiety. They were both quite young and quite callow and stood little chance with a cosmopolitan of Crabb's caliber. But there was another man of whom people spoke. His name was Heywood *Pennington*, and for three years he had been off a-soldiering in the *Philippines*. It had only been a boy-and-girl affair, of course, and most people in *Philadelphia* had forgotten it, but from his well-stored memory Crabb recalled at least one calf-love that had later grown into a veritable bull-in-the-china-shop. It was not that he didn't believe fully that *Patricia* would marry him, and it wasn't that he didn't believe in *Patricia*. It was only that he knew that for the first time in his life, his whole happiness depended upon that least stable but most wonderful of creatures, the unconscious coquette. Moreover, Mortimer Crabb believed firmly in himself, and he also believed that, married to him, Patricia would be safely fulfilling her manifest destiny.

But the Philippine soldier kept bobbing up into Crabb's background at the most inopportune moments: once when the soldier's name had been mentioned on the *Blue Wing,* and Patricia had sighed and turned her gaze to the horizon, again at a dinner at Bar Harbor, and later in Philadelphia, at the Club. Bit by bit Crabb had learned Heywood Pennington's history, from the wild college days, through his short business career to the tempestuous and scarcely honorable adventures which had led to his enlistment under a false name in the regular army three years ago. It was not a creditable history for a fellow of Pennington's antecedents, and when his name was mentioned, even the fellows who had known him longest, turned aside and dismissed him with a word.

The name of the soldier never passed between the engaged couple, and so far as Crabb was concerned, Mr. *Pennington* might never have existed.

Patricia lacked nothing which the most exacting fiancée might require. Roses and violets arrived regularly at the Wharton country place near Haverford, and in the afternoons Crabb himself came in a motor car, always cheerful, always patient, always original and amusing.

To such a wooing, placid, and ardent by turns, *Patty* yielded inevitably, and at last, late in September, consented to announce the engagement. The news was received in her own family circle with delighted amazement, for Mortimer Crabb had by this time made many friends in *Philadelphia*, and Miss Wharton had refused so many offers that her people, remembering *Pennington*, had decided that their handsome relative was destined to a life of single blessedness. They bestirred themselves at once in a round of entertainments in her honor, the first of which was a lawn party and masque at her uncle *Philip* Wharton's country place, near Bryn Mawr.

Philip Wharton never did things by halves, and society, back from the seashore and mountains, welcomed the first large entertainment which was to mark the beginning of the country life between seasons.

The gay crowds swarmed out from the wide doorways, into the balmy night, liberated from the land of matter-of-fact into a domain of enchantment. Gayly caparisoned cavaliers, moving in the spirit of the characters they represented strode gallantly in the train of their ladies whose graceful draperies floated like film from white shoulders and caught in their silken meshes the shimmer of the moonbeams. Bright eyes flashed from slits in masks and bolder ones looked searchingly into them. All of the ages had assembled upon a common meeting ground; a cinquecento rubbed elbows with an American In-

dian, Joan of Arc was cajoling a Crusader, a
nun was hazarding her hope of salvation in
flirtation with the devil, the eyes of a *Puri-
tan* maid fell before the glances of a mata-
dor. *N*othing had been spared in costume or
in setting to make the picture complete. The
music halted a moment and then swept into
the rhythm of a waltz. A murmur of delight
and like a change in the kaleidoscope the
pieces all converged upon the terrace.

It was here that a diversion occurred. A
laugh went up from a group upon the steps
and their glances were turned in one direction. Seated upon the balustrade in the glow
of the Chinese lanterns sat a tramp, drinking
a glass of punch from the refreshment table
close at hand. It was a wonderful disguise
that he wore. The shirt of some dark material, was stained and torn, the hat, of the
brown, army type, was battered out of shape,
and many holes had been bored into the
crown. The trousers had worn to the color
of dry grass and the boots were old, patched,

and yellow with mud and grime. In place
of the conventional black mask, he wore a
bandanna handkerchief tied around his brow,
with holes for the eyes. The ends of the handkerchief hung to his breast and hid his features, but under its edges could be seen a
brown ear and a patchy beard. As the crowd
watched him he lifted his glass aloft solemnly
and made the motions of drinking their
health. There was a roar of applause. A
whimsical arrogance in the pose of the
squarely-made shoulders and the tilt of the
head gave an additional interest to the som-
ber figure. He looked like a drawing from
the pages of a comic weekly, but the osten-
tation of his gesture gave him a dignity that
made the resemblance less assured. As the
people crowded around him and sought to
pierce his disguise, he got down from his
perch and strolled away into the shadows.
When the music stopped again he was sur-
rounded by a curious group, but he towered
in their center grotesque, and inscrutable. To

those who questioned him too closely he mumbled at their meddling and told them to be off. Then he tightened his belt and asked when supper would be ready.

"Are you hungry?" someone asked. He glared at the questioner.

"What kind of a tramp would I be if I wasn't hungry?" he growled, and those around him laughed again. So they took him to a table and fed him. He ate ravenously. They got him something to drink and it seemed to vanish down his throat without even touching his lips.

"Isn't he splendid?" said *Patricia* Wharton, who, with Mortimer Crabb, had just come up. "But who——? I can't think of anyone, and yet——"

The tramp looked up at her suddenly and dropped his fork upon the table.

"*Splendid,*" he cried. "*That's me. Splendid.* I sure glitter in this bunch, don't I?"

There was something irresistibly comic in the gesture with which he swept the group.

Patricia was still watching him—a puzzled expression in her eyes.

"Who is he?" she asked; but Crabb shook his head. "I haven't an idea—but he *is* clever. And look at those boots—they're the real thing. I wouldn't want to try to dance in them, though."

The tramp drained his glass—set it down on the table and wiped his mouth on the back of his hand—rose and disappeared between the palms and hydrangeas into the darkness.

For a guest in good standing the tramp then behaved strangely, for when he had reached a sheltered spot, in the bushes at the end of the English Garden, he sank at full length upon the grass and buried his head in his hands, groaning aloud. It was three years since he had seen her—three years, and yet she was just as he had seen her last. *Time* had touched her lightly, only caressing her playfully, rounding her features to matured beauty, while he—— A vision of camps, cities, skirmishes, orgies, came out of his mind in a disordered procession, all culminating in the incident which had brought him to ruin. Every detail of *that* at least was clear; the sudden rage where the bonds of patience had reached the snapping point—and then the blow. The tramp laughed outright. He could see now the smirk on the face of the drunken lieutenant as he toppled over backward and struck his head on the edge of the mahogany table. After that—irons, the court martial, the transport, Alcatraz, his chance, the friendly plank, the swim for the mainland, and freedom. He had never heard whether the man lived or died. He didn't much care. He got what was coming to him.

The tramp was a fugitive still. He had walked since morning from Malvern station, where he had been thrown off the freight train on which he had worked a ride east from Harrisburg. At Bryn Mawr he had begged a meal—the irony of it had sunk into his soul —at the back door of a country house at which he had once been a welcome guest. A gossipy chauffeur had let him into his garage for a rest and had given him a cigarette over which he had learned the recent doings in the neighborhood. The thought of venturing into *Philip* Wharton's grounds that night had entered his madcap brain while he lay in the woods along the Gulf Road, trying to make up his mind whether his tired feet would carry him the twelve miles that remained between him and the city.

Why had he returned? God knew. His feet had dragged him onward as though impelled by some force beyond his power to resist. Now that he was near the home of his boyhood it seemed as if any other place in the world would have been better. It was so real —the peaceful respectability of this country —so like Her. And yet its very peacefulness and respectability angered him. Was it nothing to have hungered and thirsted and sweated that the honor of these people and that of others like them might be preserved? Even *Patricia's* blamelessness was intolerant—reproachful. The springs of memory that had gushed forth just now at the sight of her were dried in their source. There was a dull ache, a sinking of the spirit that was almost a physical pain; but the unreasoning fever of the wayward boy, the wrenching fury of the outcast soldier were lacking, and for a long time he lay where he had fallen without moving.

CHAPTER XI

PATRICIA WHARTON stood a moment on the edge of the terrace after the dance, slipped her hand into Mortimer Crabb's arm and came down upon the path, drawing a drapery across her white shoulders.

"What is it?" asked Crabb. "You are not cold?"

"Oh, no," she said quietly. "I think I am a little tired."

"Come," he said. "There's a beautiful spot—just here." He led her across the lawn and through an opening in the trees to a garden-bench in the shadow, a spot which none of the other maskers had discovered. Through the leafy screen they could see the gay figures floating like will-o'-the-wisps across the golden lawn, but here they were quiet and unobserved. *Patricia* sank upon the bench with a sigh, while Crabb sat beside her.

"Are you happy?" he asked after awhile.

"Perfectly," she murmured. "What a beautiful party!" She placed her hand in his and moved a little closer to him, then sat listlessly, her eyes seeking the spaces between the branches where the people were. "I don't want to grow old too soon," she was saying. "The whole world is in short clothes to-night. Wouldn't it be good to be young forever?"

Crabb smiled indulgently.

"Yes," he said. "It is good to be young. But isn't it anything to take your place in the world? I want you to know all a man can do for the woman he loves. Won't you let me? Soon?" He bent over her and took the rounded arm in his strong hand. She did not withdraw it, but something told him a link of sympathy was lacking in the chain. As she did not reply he straightened and sat moodily looking before him.

"Don't think me capricious, please," she

began. "You're everything I can hope for—and yet——"

"And yet?" he repeated.

She paused a moment, then broke in, "Forgive me, won't you? I don't know what it is. Something has affected me strangely." She leaned against the back of the bench, rested her head in her hand, away from him, and Crabb turned jealously toward her.

"You were thinking—of him—of the other."

"Why shouldn't I be honest with you? I can't help it. Something has suddenly brought him into my mind. I was wondering——"

"Yes."

"I was wondering where he is now—to-night. It is so beautiful here. Everything has been done to make us happy. I was thinking that perhaps if I had written him a line I might have saved him some terrible trial. It was only a boy-and-girl affair, of course, but——"

Patricia suddenly stopped speaking, and both of them turned their heads toward the dark bank of bushes behind them.

"What was it?" she asked.

"A dead branch falling," he replied.

They listened again, but all they heard was the sound of the orchestra and the voices of the dancers.

"You're teaching me a lesson in patience," Crabb began again soberly. "I can wait, of course. I'm not jealous of *him*," he said. "I was only wondering how you could think of him at all."

"I don't think of him—not in *that* way. I believe I haven't thought of him at all—until to-night. To-night, I can't help thinking of others less fortunate than ourselves. I suppose it's only the natural thing that he should suffer. He never seemed to get things right, somehow; his point of view was always askew. He was a wild boy—but he was human."

She paused and clasped her hands before her. Crabb sat silent beside her, but his brow was clouded. When he spoke it was in a voice low and constrained.

"Do you think it kind—wise to speak of this now?"

"I was thinking that perhaps if he'd had a little luck——"

"He might have come back to you?"

Patricia turned toward him and with a swift movement took one of his hands in both of hers.

"Don't speak in that way," she pleaded. "You mustn't."

But his fingers still refused to respond to her pressure.

"If I think of him at all, it is because I have learned how great a thing is love and how much the greater must be its loss. You know," she whispered, timidly, "you know I —I love you."

"God bless you for that," he murmured.

They were so absorbed that they did not hear the sound behind them—a suppressed moan like that of an animal in pain.

"Will you forgive me?" asked the girl, at last. "It is all over now. I shall never speak of it again. I've spoiled your evening. You don't regret?"

Crabb laughed happily.

"I'll promise to be good," she said, softly. "I'll do whatever you ask me——"

"Will you marry me next month?"

"Yes," she murmured, "whenever you wish."

He took her in his arms and kissed her. They stood for some time deaf to all voices but those in their hearts. *T*here was a breaking of tiny twigs under the trees behind them and a drab figure came out into the open on the other side and vanished into the darkness by the garden wall. And as they walked back into the house neither guessed just what had happened except that some new miracle, which, really, is very old, had happened to them.

As a matter of fact, when *Patricia* announced the miracle in the form of her engagement to Mortimer Crabb a prayer of thanksgiving went up from at least three young women of her acquaintance. And though these feminine petitioners were left as much to their own devices as before the announcement, there was a certain comfort in knowing that she was out of the way—at least, that she was as much out of the way as it was possible for *Patricia* to be, bound or untrammeled. Jack Masters went abroad, Steve Ventnor actually went to work, and various other swains sought pastures new.

Ross Burnett was best man and, when the ceremony and breakfast were over, saw the happy couple off upon the *Blue Wing,* for their long Southern cruise. They offered him conduct as far as Washington, whither he was bound, but he knew from the look in their eyes that he was not wanted, and with a promise to meet them in *New* York when they returned, he waved them a good-by from the pier and took up the thread of his Government business where it had been dropped. It is not often that good comes out of villainy, and the memory of the adventure in which Crabb had involved him, often troubled his conscience. What if some day he should meet Baron Arnim or Baron Arnim's man and be recognized? At the State Department Crowthers had asked him no questions and he had thought it wise not to offer explanations. But certain it was that to that adventure alone was his present prosperity directly due. His South American mission successfully concluded, he had returned to Washington with the assurance that other and even more important work awaited him. His point of view had changed. All he had needed was initiative, and, Crabb having supplied that deficiency, he had learned to face the world again with the squared shoulders of the man who had at last found himself. The world was his oyster and he would open it how and when he liked.

It was this new attitude perhaps which enabled him to take note of the taming of Mortimer Crabb, for when he visited the bride and groom in their sumptuous house in New York, he discovered that Crabb had formed the habit of the easy-chair after dinner, and that the married life, which all his days he had professed to abhor, was the life for him. It took the combined efforts of Burnett and Patricia to dislodge him.

"He's absolutely impossible," said *Patricia*. "He says that he has solved the problem of happiness—that he has done with the world. It's so like a man," and she stamped her small foot, "to think that marriage is the end of everything when—as everyone knows—it's only the beginning. He's getting stout already, and I know, I'm positive that he is going to be bald. Won't you help me, Mr. Burnett?"

"*T*hat's a dreadful prospect—Benedick, the married man. You only need carpet slippers and a cribbage-board, Mort, to make the picture complete. Have you stopped seeking opportunities?"

"Ah, yes," drawled Crabb, "Patty is the only opportunity I ever had—at least—er— the only one worth embracing——"

"Mortimer!"

"And don't you ever go to the Club?" laughed Ross.

"Oh, no. I'm taboo there since I lived in *Philadelphia*. Besides, I'm not a bachelor any more, you know. If *Patty* only wouldn't insist on dragging me out——"

Patricia laughed.

"*Twice*, Ross, already this winter," Crabb continued. "It's cruelty, nothing less." But the perpetrator of the outrage was smiling, and she leaned forward just then and laid her hand in that of her husband, saying with a laugh, "Mort, you know we'll have to get Ross married at once."

"Me?" said Burnett, in alarm.

"Of course. A bachelor only sneers at a Benedick when he has given up hoping——"

"Oh, I say now—I'm not so old."

"Then you do hope?"

"Oh, no, I only wait—for a miracle."

"*T*his isn't the age of miracles," remarked Patty thoughtfully, "at least not miracles of that kind. How can you expect anyone to fall in love with you if you go on leaping from one end of the earth to the other. *N*o girl wants to marry a kangaroo—even a diplomatic kangaroo." She paused and examined him with her head on one side. "And yet you know you're passably decent looking——"

"Oh, thanks!"

"Even distinguished—that foreign way of wearing your mustache is really quite fetching. You'll do, I think, with some coaching."

"Will you coach me?"

"I object," interrupted Crabb, lazily.

"I will. You're quite worth marrying— I'm at least sure you wouldn't condemn your wife to her own lares and penates."

"*N*ot I. She'd get the wanderlust—or a divorce."

"Don't boast, worse vagabonds than you

have been tamed—come now, what shall she be—blonde or brunette?"

Burnett shrugged his shoulders. "I'm quite indifferent—pigment is cheap nowadays."

"Now you're scoffing."

Ross Burnett leaned back in his chair and smiled at the chandelier. Women had long ago been omitted from his list of possibilities. But *Patricia* was not to be denied.

"Married you shall be," she said with the air of an oracle, "and before the year is out. I swear it."

"But why do you want me to——"

"Revenge!" she said tragically. "You helped marry me to Mort."

And the young matron was as good as her word, though her method may have been unusual.

It came about in the following manner, and Burnett's brother and Miss Millicent Darrow were her unconscious agents. Miss Darrow had gone to the Academy Exhibit. The rooms were comfortably crowded. She entered conscious of a certain dignity and re-pose in the character of her surroundings. She brought forth her catalogue, resolutely opened it to the first page and in a moment was oblivious to the people about her. She did not belong to the great army "who know what they like." She had an instinctive perception of the good, and found herself not a little amazed at the amount of masterly work by younger men whose names she had never heard. It was an unpleasant commentary upon the mentality and taste of the set in which she moved, and she was conscious of a sense of guilt; for was she not a reflection of the shortcomings of those she was so ready to condemn? "The Plain—Evening—William Hazelton"—a direct rendering of an up-land field at dusk, between portraits by well-known men; "Sylvia—Henry Marlow"—a girl in a green bodice painted with knowledge and assurance.

In another room were the things in a high-er key—she knew them at a glance; and on the opposite wall a full-length portrait that looked like a Sargent. She was puzzled at the color, which was different from that of any man she remembered. The Sargents she knew were grouped in another room—and yet there was here the force and breadth of the master. She experienced the same perplexity—"Agatha—*Philip Burnett*," said the catalogue. She sank upon a bench before it and gave herself up to quiet rapture.

"If I were a man," she said at last, "that is how I should wish to paint, the drawing of Sargent, the poetry of Whistler, the grace of Alexander, the color of Benson. *Philip Bur-nett*," she apostrophized, "I'm a *Philistine*. Forgive me."

CHAPTER XII

IT was very pleasant under the subdued lights from above. She followed the sweep of the drapery with delighted eye, taking an almost sensuous pleasure in the relation of color and the grace of the arms and throat—the simplicity of the modeling and the admirable characterization.

She found herself repeating:

> "'And those that were good shall be happy,
> They shall sit in a golden chair;
> They shall splash at a ten-league canvas
> With brushes of comet's hair.'

"Philip Burnett, I wonder if you're good? You ought to be. I'd be good if I could paint like that. I'd work for an age at a sitting, too. How could one ever be tired making adagios in color? Oh!" she sighed, "how good it must be to amount to something!"

A procession of agreeable, vacuous faces passed before the canvas, creatures of a common fate, garbed in the uniform of convention, carrying the polite weapons of Vanity Fair, each like the others and as uninteresting. The few who wore the bright chevrons of distinction had marched with the throng for a time, but had gone back to their own. She wondered if it would really matter if she never saw them again; of course, the women —but the men. Would she care?

Was there not another life? It beckoned to her. What was *Philip* Burnett like? Could he be young and handsome as well as gifted? The vacuous faces vanished and in their place she could see this young genius— Antinous and Hercules combined—standing before this canvas living for the mere joy of work. Here was her answer. Was she to flit through enchanted gardens other people had planted, sipping only at the perfumed petals while the honey to be garnered was in plain sight?

A voice broke in just beside her:

"It's convincing, but I tell you, Burnett, the arm's too long."

"*P*erhaps. Not bad, though, for a new man. You know we Burnetts are an exceptional race."

The men moved away and the other's reply was lost in the murmur of the crowd. Miss Darrow turned to follow them with her eyes —what a big fellow he was! with an admirable profile, a straight nose, a waxed mustache, and a chin like the one on the mask of Brutus. Conceited, of course! All artists were conceited. And who was that with him —Mortimer Crabb? Yes, and there was the bride talking to the *P*endergasts.

"Why, Milly, dear!" Mrs. *P*endergast passed an incurious but observant eye over her acquaintance. "I thought you were in Aiken. What a lovely hat! Are you going to the Inghams? What will you wear? Isn't it restful here?"

Miss Darrow politely acquiesced and at-

tempted replies, but her eyes strayed toward
the Burnett portrait.

"Stunning," continued Mrs. *P*endergast.
"A new man just over. Quite too clever.
Wonderful color, isn't it? Like a ripe pome-
granate."

"Have you met him?"

"*N*o. He belongs to the Westchester Burnetts, though. Mrs. Hopkinson. So glad. Is
Frederick here?"

The agreeable lady had made of the por-
tion of the galleries in the neighborhood of
the Burnett portrait a semblance of her own
busy drawing-room. Other acquaintances
came up and Miss Darrow was soon lost in
the maze of small talk. A broad pair of
shoulders were thrust forward into her group,
and Miss Darrow found herself looking into
a pair of quizzical gray eyes which were
beaming a rather frank admiration into hers.
"Miss Darrow—Mr. Burnett," *P*atricia
Crabb was saying; and Millicent Darrow was
conscious that in a moment the new arrival

had quietly and cleverly appropriated her and was taking her to the opposite side of the room where he found for her a Winslow Homer of rocks and stormy splendor.

"Why is it," she asked, after her first enthusiasm, "that the work of the artist so seldom suggests its creator's personality?"

"The perversity of the human animal," he laughed. "*T*hat's the system of justice of the great Republic of Art, Miss Darrow. If we lose a characteristic here, we gain it somewhere else. Rather a nice balance, don't you think?"

"You hardly look the poet, Mr. Burnett—you don't mind my saying so?" she laughed. "And if you do dream, you do it with your eyes very wide open."

Mr. Burnett's brows were tangled in bewilderment. "I'm really not much given to dreaming. I'm rather busy, you know."

"It's splendid of you. You've worked long?"

"Er—yes—since I left college," he said,

the tangle in his brows suddenly unraveling. A smile now illuminated his rather whimsical eyes. Miss Darrow found herself laughing frankly into them.

"Art is long—you must be at least—thirty."

"Less," he corrected. "Youth is my compensation for not being a lawyer—or a broker."

She was conscious of the personal note in their conversation, but she made no effort to avoid it. This genius of less than thirty gave every token of sanity and good fellowship.

"Who is Agatha?" she asked suddenly.

"A—er—a friend of mine in *Paris*."

"Oh!" she said, in confusion.

And then:

"The face is of the East—the Slav—did you choose her for that character?"

"Not at all. She was—er—just—just a sitter—a commission, you know."

"How interesting!"

*T*hey had made the rounds of the room and were now facing the portrait again.

"It was lucky to have so good a model," he continued. "One doesn't always. Have you ever posed, Miss Darrow?"

"I? *N*o, never. Father has been trying to get me painted this winter. But I've been so busy—and then we're going South in two weeks—so we haven't been able to manage it."

"What a pity!" The subtle sparkle had died in his eyes, which from the shadow of their heavy lashes were regarding hers intently.

"You're very kind. Would you really like to paint me?" said Miss Darrow. "Suppose I said you should. I want my portrait done. If you make me half as wonderful as Agatha, I shall die happy. Won't you come in to-morrow at five? We can talk it over. I must be going now. *N*o, not now, to-morrow. Au revoir." She gave him her hand with a friendly nod, and threaded her way through the crowd, leaving Burnett staring at the card she had left in his hand.

On the way up-town in the machine Patricia examined him, smiling curiously.

"What a delusion you are, Ross Burnett! Railing in one moment at matrimony and in the next, tagging around like a tame bear at the heels of the first pretty girl that crosses your path."

"She *is* pretty, isn't she?" he admitted, promptly.

"And quite the rage—this is her third season you know. You seemed to be getting on very rapidly——"

"Oh, it was all a mistake," Burnett laughed. "She thought I was an artist."

"An artist? What in the world——"

"I'm going to do her portrait——"

"You!" Patricia leaned forward eagerly. "What do you mean?"

"That I'm brother *Philip*—the chap that did the Agatha. She mistook me for him, and she was so nice about it that I didn't like to interfere."

Crabb was lighting a cigarette.

"I'm afraid, my dear Ross, that the East has sapped some of your moral fiber," he said.

"It's perfectly delightful," laughed Patricia.

"But Ross can't paint——"

"I'd like to try," said Burnett.

"Fiddlesticks!"

Patricia said no more, but all the way home her face wore a smile which would not come off. The miracle had happened. Had she searched *New* York she could not have found a girl more eminently suited to Ross Burnett. *That* night Mortimer had some writing to do, but *Patricia* and her guest sat for a long while talking earnestly in the library. *They* didn't take Mortimer into their confidence, for *Patricia* had now gleefully donned the mantle her husband had so carelessly thrown aside. Here was an opportunity to make, and *Patricia* became the goddess in the machine.

CHAPTER XIII

SEVERAL days passed. Ross Burnett moved about the studio adjusting a canvas upon an easel, bringing out draperies, raising and lowering curtains, and peering into drawers and chests in a manner which betrayed an uncertain state of mind. At last he seemed to find what he was looking for—a drapery of soft gray material. This he cast over the back of the easel, walked back from it to the far side of the room where he put his head on one side and looked with half-closed eyes.

There was a clatter of the old French knocker. Burnett dropped his paint tubes and cigarette and opened the door.

"Am I late?" laughed Miss Darrow.

"You couldn't come too early," said Burnett. But he dubiously eyed the French maid who had entered bearing a huge portmanteau.

"I was so afraid to keep you waiting. You're not very angry?"

"I'm sure I've been here since dawn," he replied.

"Then let's not waste any time. Oh, isn't it charming! Where shall I go?"

He pushed open the door of the dressing room.

"I think you'll find the mirror fair," he said. "If there's anything——"

"How exciting! *No.* And I'll be out in a jiffy."

When the door was closed Burnett eyed the model-throne, the draperies, the chair, and the canvas, seeking a last inspiration before the imminent moment. He put a Japanese screen behind the chair and threw a scarlet drapery over one end of it, knocking at the rebellious folds to make them fall as he wished.

"Will I do?" asked the girl, radiantly emerging. She wore a black evening dress. The maid had thrown a filmy drapery over her which brought out the dull whiteness of the shoulders. "It is so different in the day-time," she said, coloring; "but father has always wanted it so. You know I haven't told him. It's to be a surprise."

Burnett's color responded to hers. He bowed his head. "You are charming," he murmured gallantly with a seriousness she could not fail to notice.

When Julie was dismissed to return at luncheon-time, Mr. Burnett conducted Miss Darrow to her throne and took his place before the canvas. She stood leaning easily upon the back of the chair, the lines of her slender figure sweeping down from the radiant head and shoulders into the dusky shadows behind her. She watched him curiously as he stood away from the easel to study the pose.

"If I only could—it's splendid so," he was murmuring, "but I wish you to sit."

She acquiesced without question. "I feel like a specimen," she sighed. "It's a terrible ordeal. I'm all arms and hands. M*ust* you squint?"

In Burnett's laugh all restraint was liberated to the winds.

"Of course. All artists squint. It's like the circular sweep of the thumb—a symbol of the craft."

He walked behind her and adjusted the screen, taking away the crimson drapery and putting a greyish-green one in its place.

"*T*here," he cried, "just as you are. It's stunning."

She was leaning forward with an elbow on the chair arm, her hands clasped, one slender wrist at her chin.

"Really! You're awfully easy to please— I wonder if I shall do as well as Agatha."

He took up a charcoal—looked at its end, and made a slight adjustment of the easel. "Before we begin—there's one thing I forgot." He paused. "All painters are sensitive, you know. I'm rather queerer than most. I hope you won't care." The charcoal was now making rapid gyrations upon the surface of the canvas. "I'm awfully sensitive to criticism—in the early stages. I usually manage to pull out somehow—but in the beginning— when I'm drawing, laying in the figure —I don't like my canvas seen. Sometimes it lasts even longer. You won't mind not looking, will you?"

"I see. *That's* what the grey thing is for. I don't mind in the least; only I hope it will come soon. I'm wild to see. And please smoke. I know you want to."

The grateful Burnett drew forth his cigarette-case and while his model rested busied himself among his tubes of paint, squeezing the colors out upon the palette.

"If you only knew," he sighed, "how very difficult it seems." But the large brush dipped into the paint and Burnett worked vigorously, a fine light glowing in his eyes. Miss Darrow watched the generous flow from the oil cup mingling with the colors.

"'What a lot of vermilion you use.'"

"What a lot of vermilion you use!"

"Hair," he replied. He seemed so absorbed that she said no more, and she didn't know whether to laugh or frown. Later she ventured:

"If it's carroty I'll never speak to you again. *P*lease make it auburn, Mr. Burnett."

He only worked the more rapidly. He seemed to be dipping into every color upon the palette, in the center of which had grown a brown of the color of walnut-juice. *T*his he was applying vigorously to the lower part of the canvas. When the palette was cleared he put it aside and sank back in a chair with a sigh.

"Rest," said the artist.

"I'm not in the least tired," she replied.

"But I am. It takes it out of me to be so interested."

"Does it?" She leaned back in her chair, regarding him with a new curiosity. "Do you know," she added, "you are full of surprises——"

She ignored the inquiry of his upraised brows.

"——and paint," she finished with a laugh.

He ruefully eyed a discolored thumb. "I'm awfully untidy, I know. I've always been. In *Paris* they called me Slovenly *Peter*."

"I shouldn't say that—only——"

"What?"

"Only——" she indicated several streaks of black on his grey walking-suit. "Must one always pay such a price to inspiration?"

"Jove! *That* was stupid. I always do, though, Miss Darrow." He examined the spots and touched them with the tips of his fingers. "It's paint," he finished, examining it with a placidity almost impersonal. "It doesn't matter in the least."

"And do you always smudge your face?" she asked sweetly. He looked at himself in the mirror. *T*here was a broad streak of red across his forehead. He wiped it off with a handkerchief.

"Oh, please don't laugh."

144

He sank upon the edge of the throne, and then they both laughed joyously, naturally, like two children.

"I'm an awfully lucky fellow," he said, at last. "I feel like a feudal baron with a captured princess. Here are you, that most inaccessible of persons, the Woman of Society, doomed every morning for two weeks to play Darby and Joan with a man you've known only three days. How on earth can a fellow survive seeing a girl he likes behind cups of tea! It's rough, I think. Society seems to accomplish every purpose but its avowed one. Instead of which everybody plays puss-in-the-corner. A fellow might have a chance if the corners weren't so far apart. And I, just back from abroad with all the skeins of old friendship at a loose end, walk into your circle and quietly appropriate you for a fortnight— while your other friends go a-begging."

"They haven't begged very hard," she laughed. "If they had, perhaps they might be playing Darby and Joan, too. I've never tried it before. But I think it's rather nice——" She broke off suddenly.

"Do you know, I've rested *quite* twenty minutes," she said after a moment. "Come, time is precious."

"*T*hat depends——"

She waited a moment for him to finish, but he said no more.

"How extraordinary!" she said with a pretty *mouë*. "I don't know whether I should be pleased or not."

"Can you blame me? The Forelock of *T*ime hangs too temptingly," he laughed. "Of course, if you'd rather pose——" He took up his dripping brushes with a sigh.

"Oh, indeed, I don't care," she sank back in the chair. "Only don't you think—isn't that really what I'm here for?"

"It is time to pose, Miss Darrow," he said determinately.

But she made no move to get into the position.

"I haven't complained," and she smiled at

him. "Your muse is difficult, and I'm the gainer. Really, I think I'd rather talk."

"And I'm waiting to go on with the portrait."

"I'll pose again on one condition——"

"Yes."

"*T*hat you put on overalls."

The brushes and palette dropped to his side. "*T*hat's rough on Slovenly *P*eter," he laughed. He set about squeezing the paint tubes, wiping the brush handles and edge of the palette. When the pose was over Julie appeared. The artist drew the grey drapery over the easel and helped Miss Darrow to descend.

CHAPTER XIV

THESE mornings in the studio were full of subtleties. Miss Darrow discovered that Burnett could talk upon many subjects. He had traveled much in Europe, and could even draw a bold outline for her of the East, which she had never seen. He talked little of art, and then only when the subject was introduced by his model. In the rests, which were long, he led Miss Darrow, often without her being aware of it, down pleasant lanes of thought, all of which seemed to end abruptly in the garish sunshine of personality. She did not find it unpleasant; only it seemed rather surprising the way all formality between them had been banished.

One morning there was a diversion. A clatter on the knocker and Burnett, frowning, went to the door. Miss Darrow heard a feminine voice and an exclamation. Burnett went rather hurriedly and stood outside, his hand upon the door knob. There was a murmur of conversation and a feminine laugh. She tried not to hear what was said. The hand fidgeted on the knob, but the murmur of voices continued. Miss Darrow got down from the throne and moved to the window, adjusting a stray curl as she passed.

She looked away from the mirror, then stopped suddenly and looked again. When Burnett entered she was sitting in the window-seat, looking out over the roof-tops. He was profuse in apology. She resumed the pose and the artist painted silently. "They say there's a pleasure in painting that only a painter knows," she began.

"Of course."

"Then why do we rest so often? I'm not easily deceived. The fine frenzy is lacking, Mr. Burnett—isn't it so?"

For reply he held out his paint-smudged hands.

"No—no," she went on. "You're painting

timidly with the tips of your fingers—not in the least like the 'Agatha.' I'm sure you're doing me early-Victorian."

Burnett stopped painting, looked at his canvas and laughed. "Oh, it's hardly that," he said.

"Won't you prove it?"

"How?"

"By letting me look." She rose from her chair, got down from the throne and took a rapid step or two towards the easel. But Burnett's broad shoulders barred the way.

"*Please,*" she urged.

"I can't, really."

"Why not?" She stood her ground firmly, looking up into his face, but Burnett did not move or reply.

She settled into the pose again and Burnett went mechanically to his place before the canvas. Once it seemed as if he were about to speak—but he thought better of it. He looked down at the mass of color mingled on the palette. His brush moved slowly on the canvas. At last it stopped and dropped to his side.

"I can't go on."

She dropped out of the pose. "Are you ill?"

"Oh, no," he laughed. With the setting aside of the brushes and palette, Burnett seemed to put away the shadow that had been hanging over his thoughts all the morning. He stood beside her and was looking frankly into her eyes. She saw something in his that had not been there before, for she looked away, past the chimneys and apartment houses, past the clouds, and into the void that was beyond the blue. She had forgotten his presence, and one of her hands which he held in both of his.

"*P*erhaps you understand," he said quietly. "*P*erhaps you know."

The fingers moved slightly, but on the brows a tiny frown was gathering. He relinquished her hand with a sigh and stood looking rather helplessly in the direction of the mute and pitiless easel. They were so deep in thought that neither of them heard the turning of a skeleton key in the latch and the opening of the door. The Japanese screen for a moment concealed them from the view of a gentleman who emerged into the room. Ross Burnett looked up helplessly. It was Mortimer Crabb, horror-stricken at this violation of his sanctum.

"Ross!" he said, "what on earth——"

Miss Darrow started from her chair, the crimson rushing to her cheeks, and stood drawing the lace across her shoulders.

Burnett was cool. "Miss Darrow," he asked, "you know Mr. Crabb? He's studying painting, and—er—sometimes uses this place. Perhaps——"

The words hung on his lips as he realized that Miss Darrow with an inclination of the head toward the visitor, had vanished into the dressing-room.

As the door closed words less polite came forth.

But Crabb broke in: "Oh, I say, Ross, you don't mean you've had the nerve——"

Ross Burnett's brows drew together and his large frame seemed to grow compact.

"Hush, Mort," he whispered. "You don't understand. You've made an awful mess of things. Won't you go?"

"But, my dear chap——"

"I'll explain later. But go—please!"

With a glance toward the easel Mortimer Crabb went out.

Ross Burnett closed the door, shot its bolt and put his back against it. As the clatter of Crabb's boots on the wooden stairs died away on the lower floor, he gave a sigh, folded his arms and waited.

When Miss Darrow emerged from the dressing-room ready for the street, she found him there.

"My things are in the portmanteau," she said, icily. "My maid will call for them. If you will permit me——"

But Burnett did not move.

"Miss Darrow——" he began.

"Will you let me pass?"

"I can't, Miss Darrow—until you hear. I wouldn't have had it happen for anything in the world."

"I cannot listen. Won't you open the door?"

He bowed his head as though better to receive her reproaches, but he did not move.

"Oh!" she cried, "how could you!" Her chin was raised, and she glanced scornfully at him from under her narrowed lids.

"*Please*," he pleaded, quietly. "If you'll only listen——"

She turned and walked towards the window. "Isn't it punishment enough for it all to end like this," he went on, "without making it seem as though I were worse than I am? Really, I'm not as bad as I'm painted."

It was an unfortunate phrase. An awkward silence followed it, in which he was conscious that Miss Darrow had turned sud-

denly from the window and was facing the
*T*hing upon the easel, which was now revealed to them both in all its uncompromising ugliness. From the center of a myriad
of streaks of paint something emerged.
Something in dull tones, staring like a Gor-
gon from its muddy illusiveness. To Burnett
it had been only a canvas daubed with in-
felicitous paint. *N*ow from across the room
it seemed to have put on a smug and scurri-
lous personality and odiously leered at him
from its unlovely background.

"Don't," cried Burnett. "Don't look at
the thing like that."

But the girl did not move. She stood before the easel, her head a little on one side,
her eyes upon the canvas.

"It's really not Victorian, is it?" she asked
calmly.

"You *must* listen!" cried Burnett, leaving
his post at the door. "I insist. You know
why I did this mad thing. I've told you. I'd
do it again——"

"I've no doubt you will," she put in scornfully. "It doesn't seem to have been so difficult."

"It was. The hardest thing I've ever done in my life. You gave me the chance. I took it. I won't regret it. It was selfish—brutal—anything you like. But I don't regret—nine wonderful mornings, twenty-seven precious hours—more, I hope, than you've given any man in your life." He made one rapid stride and took her in his arms. "I love you, Millicent, dear. I've loved you from the first moment—there in the picture gallery. Yes, I'd do it again. Every moment I've blessed the luck that made it possible. Don't turn away from me. You don't hate me. I know it. You couldn't help feeling a response to a love like mine." He held her close to him, raising her head at last until her lips were level with his own. But he did not touch them. She still struggled faintly, but she would not open her eyes and look at him.

"No, no, you mustn't," was all that she found strength to say.

"You can't deny it. You do—care for me. Look up at me and tell me so."

She would not look at him and at last struggled away and stood, her cheeks flaming.

"You are masterful!" she stammered. "A girl is not to be won in this fashion."

"I love you," he said. "And you——"

"I despise you," she gasped. She turned to the mirror, and rearranged her disordered hair.

"Don't say that. Won't you forgive me?"

She sank on the model stand and buried her face in her hands. "It was cruel of you —cruel."

The sight of her distress unnerved him and gave him for the first time a new view of the enormity of his offense. It was her pride that was wounded. It was the thought of what Mortimer Crabb might think of her that had wrought the damage. He bent over her, his fingers nearly touching her, yet restrained by a delicacy and a new tenderness begotten by the thought that it was he alone who had caused her unhappiness.

"Forgive me," he whispered. "I'm sorry."

And she only repeated. "What can he think of me? What can he think?"

Burnett straightened, a new thought coming to him. It seemed like an inspiration—a stroke of genius.

"Of course," he said, calmly, "you're hopelessly compromised. He must think what he pleases. There's only one thing to do."

She arose and breathlessly asked, "What *can* I do? How can I——"

"Marry me—at once."

"Oh!"

She spoke the word slowly—wonderingly—as if the idea had never occurred to her before. He had left the way to the door unguarded, but instead she walked toward the window, and looked out over the roof-tops. To Burnett the silence was burdened with meaning, and he broke it timorously.

"Won't you—won't you, Millicent, dear?"

Her voice trembled a little when she replied: "There is one thing more important than that—than anything else in the world to me."

At her side his eyes questioned mutely.

"And that?" he asked at last.

"My reputation," she whispered.

He stood a second studying her face, for his happiness grew upon him slowly. But behind the crooked smile which was half-hidden from him, he caught the dawn of a new light that he understood. He took her in his arms then, and wondered how it was that he had not kissed her when her lips had been so close before. But the new wonder that came to them both made them willing to forget that there had ever been anything else before.

Later, Ross, unable to credit his good fortune and marveling at the intricacies of the feminine mind, asked her a question. Her reply caused him more amazement:

"*Poor*, foolish, Slovenly *Peter*! I saw it by accident in the mirror a week ago."

So it was Mortimer Crabb after all who made the opportunity; for Miss Darrow smilingly admitted that had it not been for his abrupt entrance at that precise psychological moment, she should now have been in Aiken and Ross on the way to the Antipodes. But *Patricia* was doubly happy; for had she not circumvented her own husband in opening the studio he had forsworn, the veritable chamber of Bluebeard which had been bolted against her? Had she not browsed away among the gods of his youth to her heart's content and made that sacred apartment the vestibule of *Paradise* for at least two discontented mortals whose hearts were now beating as one?

CHAPTER XV

AFTER this first success, *Patricia* was filled with the spirit of altruism, and winter and summer went out upon the highways and byways seeking the raw material for her fateful loom. She was *Puck*, *Portia* and *Patricia* all rolled into one. *There* were Stephen Ventnor and Jack Masters, whom she still saw occasionally, but they only sighed and even refused to dine at the Castle of Enchantment. She thought sometimes of Heywood *Pennington*, too, and often found herself wondering how the world was faring with him, hoping that some day chance would throw him in her way. The old romance was dead, of course. But what an opportunity for regeneration!

Meantime she had much to do in keeping up her establishment, many friends to make in *New* York, many social duties to perform.

She spent much time with her husband over the plans of the country place he was building on Long Island, which was to be ready for occupancy late in the following spring. Mortimer Crabb had formed a habit of going down town for a part of every day at least, and if he really did no work he created an impression of stability which was rather surprising to those who had known him longest. The Crabbs were desirable acquaintances in the married set, and before two years had passed, *Patricia* made for herself an enviable reputation as a hostess and dinner guest, to say nothing of that of a model wife. Not a cloud larger than a speck had risen upon the matrimonial horizon and their little bark sailed steadily forward propelled by the mildest of breezes upon an ocean that was all made up of ripples and sunshine. Mortimer Crabb loved abundantly, and *Patricia* was contented to watch him worship, while she shaped the course to her liking.

There were still times, however, when she

sat and watched the flames of the library fire while she stirred up the embers of romance. Few women who have been adored as *Patricia* had been are willing too abruptly to shut the door upon the memory of the might-have-beens. The coquette in her was dying hard—as it sometimes does in childless women. She still liked the attentions to which she had been accustomed, and her husband saw that she was constantly amused—provided with clever men from his clubs as dance partners for the *Phila*-delphia girls who visited them. Stephen Ventnor, who was selling bonds down-town, had been persuaded at last to forget his troubles and now came frequently to dinner. There was nothing *Patricia* wanted, it seemed, except something to want.

One day, quite by chance, she met another one of the might-have-beens upon the street. She did not know him at first, for he now wore a small moustache and the years had not passed as lightly over his head as they had over hers. She felt her way barred by a tall figure, and before she knew it, was shaking hands with Heywood *Pennington.*

"*Patty,*" he was saying, "don't you know me? Does four years make such a difference?" A warm tint rose and spread unbidden from *Patricia's* neck to temples. It angered her that she could not control it, but she smiled at him and said that she was glad to see him.

*T*ogether they walked up the Avenue, and, as they went, she questioned and he told her his story. *N*o recriminations passed. He made it plain to her that he was too glad to see her for that. He was in business, he said vaguely, and in the future was to make *N*ew York his home. So, when she took leave of him, *Patricia* asked the prodigal to call. It will be apparent to anyone that there was nothing else to do.

Mortimer Crabb received the information at the dinner table that night with a changeless expression.

"I'm sure if you want Mr. *Pennington*

here, he'll be welcome," he said with a slow smile. "He's a very, very old friend of yours, isn't he, *Patty?*"

"Oh, yes—since school days," she said, quietly. And she blushed again, but if Crabb noticed, it was not apparent, for he immediately busied himself with his soup.

"He used to be such a nice boy," said Patricia. "But I'm afraid he got pretty wild and——"

"Yes," put in her husband, a little dryly. "I've heard something about him."

She glanced at him quickly, but he did not look up and she went on:

"I thought it would be nice if we could do a little something for him, give him a lift, introduce him to some influential people——"

"Make an opportunity for him, in short," said Crabb.

"Er—yes. He has had a pretty hard time, I think."

"I shouldn't be surprised," said Crabb, "most people do."

Patricia foresaw an opportunity such as she had never had before, and a hundred plans at once flashed into her pretty head for the prodigal's regeneration. First, of course, she must kill the fatted calf, and she therefore planned at once a dinner party, at which Mr. Pennington should meet some of her intimate friends, Dicky Bowles and his wife, the Burnetts, who were on from Washington, the Charlie Chisolms and her sister *Penelope.* For reasons of her own Stephen Ventnor was not invited.

Patricia presided skilfully with an air of matronly benevolence not to be denied and dextrously diverted the conversation into channels strictly impersonal. So that after dinner, while Charlie Chisolm was still talking rifle-bores with Mortimer, *Patricia* and Heywood *Pennington* went into the conservatory to see the new orchids.

That was the first of many dinners. Patricia invited all the eligible girls of her acquaintance, one after another, and sat them next to Mr. *P*ennington in an apparent endeavor to supply the deficiency she had caused in that gentleman's affections. But new orchids came continually to the conservatory, and *P*atricia was not loath to show them. Then followed rides in the motor car when Crabb was down-town, and shopping expeditions when Crabb was at the club, for which Patricia chose Heywood *P*ennington as her escort, and whatever Mortimer Crabb thought of it all, he said little and looked less.

But if her husband had been willing to worship blindly before he and *P*atricia had been engaged, marriage had cleared away some of the nebulæ. He had learned to look upon his wife as a dear, capricious being, and with the abounding faith and confidence of amply proportioned men he was willing to believe that Patricia, like Cæsar's wife, was above suspicion. He was quite sure that she was foolish. But *P*atty's little finger foolish was more important to Mortimer than a whole Minerva.

Mr. Pennington's ways were not Crabb's

ways, however, and the husband learned one day, quite by chance, of an incident that had happened in *New* York which confirmed a previous impresson. He went home a little sombre, for that very night Mr. *Pennington* was to dine again at his house.

After dinner *Patricia* and *Pennington* vanished as usual into the conservatory and were seen no more until it was time for *Patricia's* guests to go. The husband lingered moodily by the fire after the door had closed upon the last one, who happened to be the might-have-been.

"*Patty*," he began, "don't you think it a little—er—inhospitable——"

"Oh, Mort," *Patricia* broke in, "don't be tiresome."

But Mortimer Crabb had taken out his watch and was examining it with a judicial air.

"Do you know," he said, calmly, "that you've been out there since ten? I don't think it's quite decent."

It was the first time her husband had used exactly this tone, and *Patricia* looked at him curiously, then pouted and laughed.

"Jealous!" she laughed, and blowing him a kiss flew upstairs, leaving her husband still looking into the fire. But he did not smile as he usually did when this was her mood, and in her last backward glance *Patricia* did not fail to notice it. Instead of following her, Mortimer Crabb lit a cigar and went over to his study. Perhaps he should have spoken more severely to *Patricia* before this. He had been on the point of it a dozen times. Gossip had dealt with *Pennington* none too kindly, but Crabb didn't believe in gossip and he did believe in his wife.

He finished his cigar and then lit another while he tried to think the matter out, until, at last, *Patricia*, a pretty vision in braids and lace, came pattering down. He heard the footfalls and felt the soft hands upon his shoulders, but did not turn his head. He knew what was to come and had not the humor or the art to compromise. *Patricia,* with quick divination, took her hands away and went around by the fire where she could look at her husband.

"Well," she said, half defiantly. Crabb replied without raising his eyes from the fire.

"*Patty,*" he said quietly, "you mustn't ask Mr. *Pennington* to the house." *Patricia* looked at him as though she had not heard aright. But she did not speak.

"You must know," he went on, "that I've been thinking about you and Mr. *Pennington* for some time, but I haven't spoken so plainly before. You mustn't be seen with Mr. *Pennington* again."

He rose and knocked his cigar ashes into the chimney and then turned to face his wife. *Patricia's* foot was tapping rapidly upon the fender while her figure presented the picture of injured dignity.

"It is preposterous—impossible," she gasped, "I'm going to ride with him to-morrow afternoon."

And then after a pause in which she eagerly scanned her husband's face, she broke forth into a nervous laugh: "Upon my word, Mort, I believe you *are* jealous."

"*P*erhaps I am," said Crabb, slowly, "but I'm in earnest, too. Do what I ask, *P*atricia. Don't ride to-morrow——"

"And if I should refuse——"

Crabb shrugged his broad shoulders and turned away.

"It would be too bad," he said, "that's all."

"But how can you do such a thing," she cried, "without a reason—without any excuse? Why, Heywood has been here every day for——" and then broke off in confusion.

Crabb smiled rather grimly, but he generously passed the opportunity by.

"Every reason that I wish—every excuse that I need. Isn't that enough?"

"*N*o, it isn't—I refuse to believe anything about him." Crabb looked at his wife sombrely.

"*T*hen we'd better say no more. Your attitude makes it impossible for me to argue the question. Good-night." He opened the door and stood waiting for her to go out. She hesitated a moment and then swept by him, her very ruffles breathing rebellion.

The next morning he kissed her good-bye when she was reading her mail.

"You'll write him, *Patty*, won't you?" he said, as he went out.

"Yes—yes," she answered, quickly, "I will —I'll write him."

Patricia did write to him. But it was not at all the sort of a letter that Crabb would have cared to see.

Dear Heywood [it ran], something has happened, so can't ride to-day. Meet me near the arch in Washington Square at three. Until then—

As ever,

P.

CHAPTER XVI

PATRICIA awoke rudely and with an appalling sense that she had made a shocking fool of herself. Heywood Pennington suddenly vanished out of her life as completely as though Fifth Avenue had opened and swallowed him. Very suddenly he had left New York, they said. And upon her breakfast tray one morning Patricia found the following in a handwriting unfamiliar and evidently disguised:

March 12, 19—

Mrs. Mortimer Crabb,
    Dear Madam:
    I have in my possession twenty-one letters and notes written by you to Mr. Heywood Pennington, formerly of Philadelphia. Kindly acknowledge receipt of this communication and bring to this office, in person, on Wednesday of next week, five thousand dol-

lars in cash or the letters will be mailed to Mr. Crabb.

(Signed) JOHN DOE,

Care of Fairman and Brooke,

No. —— Liberty Street.

There in her fingers it flaunted its brutality. What could it mean? Her letters? To Heywood *Pennington*? Why—they were only notes—harmless little records of their friendship. What had she said? How had this odious Doe——?

It was a week since she had seen the prodigal. *T*hey had quarreled some days ago, for Mr. *P*ennington's lazy humor had turned to a reckless unconvention which had somewhat startled her. Her secret declaration of independence had led her a little out of her depth, and she began to feel more and more like the child with the jam-pot—only the jam-pot was out of all proportion to real jam-pots and the smears seemed to defy the most generous use of soap and water. *T*his borrible Doe was the neighbor's boy who told, and

Mortimer Crabb was suddenly invested with a newly-born parental dignity and wisdom. Mort! It made her shudder to think of her husband receiving those letters. She knew him so well and yet she knew him so little. She felt tempted to throw all else to the winds and make a full confession—of what? of a childish ingenuousness—which confession would magnify a hundred-fold. What had she to confess? Meetings in the *Park?* Her face burned with shame. It would have seemed less childish if her face had burned with shame at things a little more tangible. Lunches in out-of-the-way restaurants, innocent enough in themselves, whose only pleasure was the knowledge that she took them unpermitted. She knew that she deserved to be stood in the corner or be sent to bed without her supper, but she quailed at the thought of meeting her husband's eye. She knew that he could make it singularly cold and uncompromising.

And the letters. Why hadn't Heywood

burned them? And yet why should he have? *Pennington's* ideas of a compromising position she realized, with some bitterness, differed somewhat from hers. And she knew she *couldn't* have written anything to regret. She tried to think, and a phrase here and there recurred to her. *Perhaps Mort* might know her well enough to guess how little they meant— but perhaps he didn't. Words written to another were so desperately easy to misunderstand.

How could these letters have fallen into the hands of a stranger? The more she thought of it the more impenetrable became the mystery. How could this villainous Doe have guessed her identity? A few of these letters were signed merely "*Patty*," but most of them were not signed at all. It was dreadful to be insulted with no redress at any hand. Five thousand dollars! The very insignificance of the figures made her position worse. Was this the value of her reputation? *T*ruly her fortunes had sunk to their lowest ebb. She tried to picture John Doe, a small ferret of a man with heavy eyes, red hair, and a rumpled shirt-front, sitting in a dingy office up three flights of stairs, fingering her little scented notes with his soiled fingers. Oh, it was horrible—horrible! Yet how could she escape? Would she not tarnish her soul still more by paying the wretched money—Mort's money— in forfeit of her disobedience to him? Every instinct revolted at the thought. Wouldn't it be better after all to throw herself upon Mort's mercy? She knew now how much bigger and better he was than anything else in the world. She loved him now. She knew it. There wouldn't ever be any more might-have-beens. She longed to feel his protecting arms about her and hear his quiet steady voice in her ears, even though it was to scold her for the mere child that she was. His arms seemed the greater sanctuary now—now that she was not sure that they ever could be opened to her. Still clasping the letter she buried her face in the pillows of her couch and wept.

That night she sent down word that she had a headache, but a night's rest did wonders. A cheerful, smiling person descended on Crabb in the midst of his morning coffee.

"What! *Patty!* At the breakfast table? Will the wonders never cease?"

"I didn't come to breakfast, Mort. I wanted to see you before you went out."

Crabb smiled over the top of his coffee cup.

"What is it, *Patty?* A hat bill or an opera cloak? I'm prepared. *Tell* me the awful worst."

"Don't, Mort—please. I can't bear you facetious. It's—er—about Madame Jacquard's bill and some others. *They've* gotten a little large and she—she wants me to help her out to-day—if I can—if you can—and I told her I would——"

Crabb was wrapped in contemplation of his muffin. But he allowed his wife to struggle through to the end. *Then* he looked up a little seriously from under heavy brows.

"Um—er—how much, *Patty?* A thousand? I think it can be managed——"

"No, Mort," she interrupted, tremulously, "you see I have had to get so many things of late—we've been going out a great deal you know—a lot of other things you wouldn't understand."

"Oh! *P*erhaps I might."

"No—I—I'm afraid I've been rather extravagant this winter. I didn't tell you but I —I've used u*p* my allowance long—ever so long ago."

Mortimer Crabb's brows were now really menacing.

"It seems to me——" he began. But she interrupted him at once.

"I know I ought to be called a beggar on horseback, because I really have ridden rather—rather fast this winter——"

"Two thousand?" he questioned.

"No, Mort, you see, it isn't only the dresses and the hats. I'm afraid I've been losing more than I should have lost at auction."

"Bridge!" he said, pitilessly, "I thought
——"

"Yes—bub—bridge."

"I thought my warning might be sufficient.
I'm sorry——"

"So am I," she whispered, her head lowered, now thoroughly abased. "I am not going to play any more."

"How much—three thousand?" he asked
again.

"No," she said, desperately, "more. I'm
afraid it will take five thousand dollars to pay
everything."

"*Phew!*" he whistled. "How in the name
of all that's expensive——"

"Oh, I don't know——" helplessly, "money
adds up so fast—I suppose that father
might help me if you can't—but I didn't
want to ask him if I could help it; you know
he——"

"Oh, no," said Crabb, with a sudden move
of the hand. "It can be managed, of course,
but I admit I'm surprised—very much sur-

prised that you haven't thought fit to take me closer into your confidence."

"I'm sorry, Mort," she muttered, humbly. "It won't happen again."

Crabb pushed back his chair and rose. "Oh, well, don't say anything more about it, *Patty*. It must be attended to, of course. Just give me a list of the items and I'll send out the checks."

"But, Mort, I'd like to——"

"I'll just stop in at Madame Jacquard's on the way uptown and——"

Patty started up and then sank back weakly.

"Oh, Mort, dear," she faltered, "it isn't worth while. It would be so much out of your way——"

"Not a bit," said Crabb, striding cheerfully to the door. "It's only a step from the subway, and then I can come on up the Avenue——"

But *Patricia* by this time had fastened tightly upon the lapels of his coat, and was looking half tearfully up into his face.

"I—I want to see Madame about some things she hasn't sent up yet—I must go there to-day. I'll—I'll tell her, Mort, and then if you'll arrange it, I'll just send it to her to-morrow."

Mortimer Crabb looked into the blue eyes that she raised to his and relented.

"All right," he said, "you shall have your own way." And then, with the suspicion of a smile, "Shall I make a check to your order?"

"To—to mine, Mort—it always makes me feel more important to pay my bills myself—and besides—the bub—bridge, you know."

When *Patricia* heard the front door shut behind her husband, she gave a great sigh and sank on the divan in a state of utter collapse.

The next day *Patricia* dressed herself in a plain, dark skirt, a long grey coat and wore two heavy veils over an unobtrusive sailor hat. In her hand she clutched a small hand satchel containing the precious check and the odious letter of John Doe. First she went to the bank and converted the check into crisp thousand dollar notes. *T*hen walking rapidly she took the elevated for that unknown region which men call down-town. *T*here was little difficulty in finding the place. The narrow doorway she had imagined was wide—even imposing, and an Irish janitor with a cheerful countenance, was sweeping the pavement and whistling. It was not in the least Dickens-ish, or Machiavellian. The atmosphere was that of a very cheerful and modern *N*ew York and *P*atricia's spirits revived. A cleanly boy in buttons ran the elevator.

But as the elevator shot up, *P*atty's heart shot down. She had hoped there would be stairs to climb. The imminence of the visit filled her with alarm, and before she realized it, she was deposited—a bundle of quivering nerves, before the very door. Gathering her shattered forces together, she knocked timorously and entered. It was a cheerful room with a bright carpet and an outlook over the river. A small boy who sat inside a wooden railing, sprang up and came forward.

"I wish to see Mr. Doe," stammered *Patty*, "Mr. John Doe."

"Must be a mistake," said the youth. "*T*his is Fairman & Brookes, Investments. *N*obody that name here, ma'am."

At that moment an elderly man of very proper appearance came forward from an inner office.

"Mrs. Crabb?" he inquired, politely. "*T*hat will do, Dick, you may go inside," and then rather quizzically: "You wished to see Mr. —er—Mr.—Doe? Mr. John Doe? I think he was expecting you. If you'll wait a moment I'll see," and he entered a door which led to another office.

*P*atricia dropped into a chair by the railing completely baffled. *T*his villainous creature expected her! How could he expect her? It was only Friday and the appointment was not until the Wednesday of the following week. She looked at her surroundings, trying to find a flaw in their prosperous garb of respectability. *T*hat such rascality could exist under the guise of decent business! And the benevolent person who had carried her name might very properly serve upon the vestry of St. ——'s church! *T*ruly there were depths of iniquity in this vile community of business people that her little social plummet could never seek to sound. The little red-headed man with the ferret eyes had vanished from her mind. In his place she saw a type even more alarming—the sleek, well-groomed man with dissipated eyes that she and Mort had often seen dining at popular restaurants. Her mission would not be as easy to accomplish as it had seemed. Her speech to the ferret-eyed man which she had so carefully rehearsed had gone completely from her mind. What she should say to this other man, whom she both loathed and feared, her vagrant wits refused to invent. So in spite of a brave poise of the head she sat in a kind of syncope of dismay, and awaited—she knew not what.

The benevolent vestryman returned smiling. "Mr. Doe has just come in, Mrs. Crabb. If you'll kindly come this way." He opened the door and stood aside with an old-world courtliness that all but disarmed her. He followed her into the inner corridor and opened another door, smiling the while, and *Patricia*, trembling from head to foot, yet resolute, went in, while the elderly person carefully closed the door behind her. A tall figure in an overcoat and soft hat was bending over the fireplace upon the opposite side of the room adjusting a log.

"Mr. Doe?" came in a small, muffled voice from behind *Patricia's* veil.

The man at the fireplace still poked at the logs and made no move to take off his hat.

"The brute—the utter brute," thought *Patricia*—and then aloud, "Mr. Doe, I believe."

"Yes, madam," said a voice at last. "I'm John Doe—what can I do for you?"

"I came about the letters—the letters, you know, you wrote me about. I am prepared to—to redeem them."

"H—m," growled the overcoat. "It's Crabb, isn't it? Mrs. Crabb? I'm always getting the Cobb and Crabb letters mixed—six of one and half a dozen of the other——"

"I beg pardon," faltered *Patty.*

"Cases very similar. Bad man—good woman. *T*rusting husband—hey? Well," he muttered brutally, "did you bring the money?"

"It is here," said *Patricia,* trembling. "Now the letters—and let me go."

The man moved slowly toward a desk against the wall with his back still turned, took out a package, rose and, turning, handed it to *Patricia.*

Had her gaze not been fixed so eagerly upon the handwriting on the package she could not have failed to note the smiling gray eyes above the upturned coat collar.

"Why, it is sealed and addressed to me!" she cried, in surprise. "The package hasn't even been opened."

"I never said it had," said the man in the

13 187

overcoat, removing his hat. "I didn't want
to read the stuff, *Patty*."

The package fell to the floor amid the flut-
tering bills. *Patricia's* knees trembled and
she would have fallen had not a pair of strong
arms gone about her and held her up.

"It's only Mort, *Patty*," said a voice.
"Don't you understand? It's all been a de-
ception and mistake. *T*here isn't any John
Doe. It's only your husband——"

"Oh, how could you, Mort?" sobbed *Patri*-
cia. "How could you be so hard—so—so
cruel?"

Crabb's answer was to push the veil back
from his wife's face and kiss away her tears.
She did not resist now and sank against him
with a restful sigh that told him more than
any words could do the full measure of her
penitence. But in a moment she started up
pale and wide-eyed.

"But this office—these people—do they
know——"

"Bless you, no," laughed Crabb. "Fairman's a sort of business associate of mine. I only borrowed his private office for an hour or so. He thinks it is a practical joke. It was—is—a cruel one——"

"But he'll guess——"

"Oh, no, he won't," laughed Crabb.

Patricia's gaze fell quietly upon the floor where the bills and the package still lay in disordered confusion.

"And the letters—you never even read them?"

"Oh, *Patty*," said her husband, "I didn't want to read 'em."

"Can you ever forgive me, Mort?" She broke away from him, bent to the floor, picked up the package, and broke the seal.

"But you *shall* read them, Mort," she cried, her face flaming, "every last silly one of them."

But Crabb's hands closed over hers and took the package gently from her. His only answer was to throw the papers into the fire.

"Oh, Mort," she murmured, horrified,

"what have you done—you might believe *anything* of me now."

"I shall" he chuckled, "that's your penance."

"*Please*, Mort—there's time yet—just read a few——"

Crabb poked vigorously at the fire.

"Oh, Mort, it's inhuman! You only knew Heywood *Pennington*——"

"Sh——" said Crabb, putting his hand over her lips. "*No* names——"

"But he——"

"*No*, no." And then, after a pause, "He wasn't even a might-have-been, *Patty*." She said no more. They sat hand in hand watching the record of *Patricia's* foolishness go up in smoke. And when the last scrap had vanished, he sprang cheerfully to his feet and picked up the scattered bills.

"Come, *Patty*, luncheon! And after that" —Mortimer Crabb stopped again and blinked quizzically at the fire—"hadn't we better keep your engagement—with Madame Jacquard?"

CHAPTER XVII

THUS ended the might-have-beens. And the thing that *Patricia* had taken to be the phantom of romance went up in the smoke of John Doe's fire. Mortimer Crabb never volunteered any information as to how he got the letters, nor any information as to what became of Heywood *Pennington*. For one horrible moment the thought crossed *Patricia's* brain that perhaps there had never been any letters of hers in the package her husband had burned, but she dismissed it as once as reflecting unpleasantly upon the quality of her intelligence. But one thing was sure, she now had an adequate understanding of the mind of her husband. It was the only misunderstanding they had ever had and *Patricia* knew there would never be another. Mr. *Pennington* did not appear again and so far as this veracious history is concerned, after his departure from *New York*, may have gone at once to Jericho. Patricia ceased to think of him, not because he was not present, but because thinking of him reminded her that she had been a fool, and no woman with the reputation for cleverness which *Patricia* possessed, could afford to make such an admission even to herself. She was now sure of several things—that she loved Mortimer Crabb with all her heart—and that she would never all her life long love anyone else. She might flirt, yes—nay more, she *must* flirt. What was the use spending one's life in bringing an art to the perfection *Patricia* had attained and then suddenly forswearing it? Fortunately her husband did not require that of her. He never quite knew what she was going to do next, but he never really mistrusted her. And to *Patricia's* credit it may be said that she never caused pain and that if she flirted—she sometimes did—it was in a good cause.

The building of the country place had gone

forward during the winter, and early summer found them installed there. Beginning with the housewarming, which was memorable, guests came and went and upon them all Patricia practiced her altruism which, since the adventure with John Doe, had taken a somewhat different character. Yet even among these she found work for her busy hands to do.

It happened that among their guests the Crabbs had staying with them as a remnant of the housewarming party a young girl who, because she was only a little younger than Patricia in years, but centuries younger in knowledge of the world, had become one of her most treasured friends.

Little Miss *North* loved her, too—looked up to her as the ignorant do to the wise, and when her engagement to the Baron DeLaunay was announced Aurora came and told *Patricia* even before she told her family. Yet Patricia's shrewd mind found something wrong and she urged the girl to come and join her housewarming for the sole reason of finding out the true inwardness of the engagement, and perhaps, too—who shall say?—to practice her arts again.

After a day or two of mild questioning, of studying, of watching, she began to see light.

Then she invited the Baron for a week end, and made certain preparations.

Then she waited his arrival with her nerves tingling.

She met her husband and the Baron at the steps as they ascended from the machine which brought them from the station.

"Ah monsieur! so glad! I was wondering if you'd be here in time for tea."

"Wild horses could not have detained me longer, from a glimpse of your *beaux yeux,* Madame."

He bent forward with a handsome gesture and kissed the tips of *Patricia's* fingers, but she laughed gaily.

"Don't waste pretty speeches, Baron. Besides——" she paused significantly and pointed toward the door through which her husband's shoulders had disappeared, "she is there," she finished.

"*Hélas!*" The Frenchman shrugged his shoulders expressively; then straightened and showed his teeth in a smile.

"Since my speeches are wasted, I will follow you in, Madame."

Patricia paused.

"All the world loves a lover—even I——"

"Yes—yes——"

"If I could be sure that you loved——"

"You?"

"Her," sternly.

He shrugged again, "Ah, yes—I love her—of course! Why, otherwise, should I wish to marry her?"

"I wonder," slowly, "why you speak of my *beaux yeux?*" she said thoughtfully.

"Because I cannot help it——"

"A lover should be blind," she put in.

"Like a husband?" he asked, significantly.

"Like a wife," she corrected, soberly.

He followed her indoors, where Aurora met them at the door of the library.

"Tea, Aurora," she announced. "Will you pour it? Mort and I will be in in a moment."

She hovered in the doorway insistently until she saw DeLaunay safely seated on the davenport at the tea-table by Aurora's side, and only then she departed in the direction of the smoking room.

Mortimer Crabb was drinking a glass of whiskey and water. At the sound of his wife's voice he turned.

"Did you get it, Mort?" she asked.

For reply he fumbled in the pockets of his dust-coat and brought forth a small package.

"Oh, yes. Here it is. Pretty insignificant affair to make such a fuss about," and he handed it to her.

"It's the little things that mean the most, my dear husband—like that," she said significantly, "and this," and she kissed him for his reward.

He held her away from him and looked at her good-humoredly—the quizzical humor that was characteristic of him.

"You never kiss me unless you're up to some mischief, *Patty*."

"*T*hen you ought to be glad I'm mischievous, Mort. It's an ill wind that blows nobody any good."

"H—m. Why all the mystery? Can't you tell a fellow?"

She shook her head.

"No."

"Why not?"

"Because then you don't know as much as I do."

"Why shouldn't I?" he protested. "I'm your husband."

"Because if you knew as much as I do——" She paused. "You know, Mort, it's only the ignorant husband who's entirely, blissfully happy."

"I'm not so sure about that," he laughed.

"Aren't you happy, Mort?" she asked.

"Ah, hang it, yes. But——"

"*T*hen there's nothing left to be said," and she kissed him again.

"I can't understand——"

She laid resisting fingers on his arm.

"Of course you can't. *T*hat's one of your charms, Mort, dear. It's much better for a woman to be misunderstood. The husband who 'understands' his wife is on the highway to purgatory. Ask no more questions. If I answer them I surely will lie to you."

"What the deuce can Daggett and McDade be doing for you. *T*hey're job-printers. *T*hey don't engrave your cards or stationery or anything——"

"N——o," with a rising inflection.

"Well—what?"

"I needed some printing."

"Well, why not go to *T*iffany's? The idea of your sending me away over on the East side——"

"*T*hey're such adorable printers, Mort."

"Who ever heard of a printer being adorable? Fudge! What's the game now? Can't you tell a fellow?"

"*No*," firmly.

Crabb always recognized the note of finality in his wife's voice, so he merely shrugged his shoulders and followed her with his eyes as she blew another kiss in his direction and vanished up the stairs.

In the privacy of her own room *Patricia* did some cryptic things with newspapers, a pair of scissors, and the package from the adorable printers, and when she had finished, she folded up the newspapers, with their mysterious contents, including the scissors, and with a fleeting glance at herself in the mirror, went down stairs.

She entered the library noiselessly and after a glance at her guests at the tea-table, she slipped her package into the drawer of the library table and joined them.

"How envious you make me—you two," she sighed, sinking into a chair, "you're so satisfied with yourselves—and with each other."

DeLaunay smiled and fingered his tea-cup. "Would you have it otherwise?" he asked.

"Oh, no," she said lightly, "I'm a professional nursery governess to polite and well-meaning persons of opposite sexes. Nursery governesses are not permitted emotions or opinions of any kind, my dears."

"But even nursery governesses are human, I am told," said DeLaunay, showing his white teeth.

"Are they? My governesses never were. They were all inhuman—like me. The sight of youthful license arouses all my professional instincts. That's why I'm in such demand by despairing mothers of romantic heiresses."

"*Patty!* you're horrid." Aurora's heavily lidded eyes opened wide. "I'm not romantic —not in the least—and I'm *not* an heiress —"

"Oh," said *Patricia.*

"At least," Aurora amended, "not in the modern sense. But it wouldn't matter to Louis or to me if we—really had to work for our living. I'm so anxious to be of some use in the world. Oh, we've planned that already, haven't we, Louis?"

"Yes," said DeLaunay, crisply, with a glance of defiance in his eye for *Patricia*. "We have planned that."

Patricia's lips twisted, but she said nothing.

"I sometimes think, *Patty*," went on Aurora, "that you're a little unsympathetic. Won't you really like to see us married?"

Patricia laughed. "Oh, yes—but **not to** each other."

"Why not?"

"You're too much in love, dear, for one thing. *C'est si bourgeois—n'est-ce-pas, Baron?* Things are arranged better in France?"

He shrugged his shoulders.

'Your customs in America are very pleasant ones," he replied, imperturbably. "I am indeed fortunate to find myself so much in accord with them."

Aurora gave him a rapturous glance for re-

ward, and he took her fingers in his in calm
defiance of his pretty hostess.

Patricia put down her finished tea-cup with
a laugh and rose.

"*Then* I can't dismay you—either of
you?"

Aurora smiled scornfully.

"*Not* in the least—can she, Louis?"

"Not in the least," he repeated.

"Oh, very well, your blood upon your own
heads."

"Or in our hearts, Madame," corrected De-
Launay, with a bow.

"Come, Aurora," smiled *Patricia*, "it's
time to dress."

Patricia spent some time and some thought
upon her toilet. Deep sea-green was her
color, for it matched her eyes, which to-night
were ·unfathomable. In the midst of her
dainty occupation she turned her head over
her shoulder and called her husband. Mortimer Crabb appeared in the door of his dress-

ing-room which adjoined, one side of his face shaved, the other white with lather.

"What is it?" he mumbled.

Patricia contemplated the back of her head at the dressing-table by the aid of a hand mirror, removed the hairpins one by one from her mouth and deliberately placed them before she replied.

"Mort," she said, slowly, "I want you to take Aurora out for a ride in the motor——"

"To-night! Oh, I say, *Patty*——"

"To-night," she said, firmly. "I'll arrange it. It will be dark and you're going to lose your way——"

"How do you know I am?"

"Because I tell you so, stupid! You've *got* to lose your way—for three hours."

He looked at her shrewdly.

"What's up now? *T*ell me, won't you? I'm tired of rolling over and playing dead. I am. Besides, what can I do with that girl for three hours?"

"Oh, I don't care," said *Patricia*. "*T*ell her

stories—romantic ones. She likes those. Anything—make love to her if you like."

"So DeLaunay can make love to *you*," peevishly. "I see. I'm not going to stand for it. I'm not any too keen on that fellow as it is. He's neglecting Aurora shamefully——"

"It *is* careless of him, isn't it?" she said, tilting her head back to get another angle on her head-dress.

Crabb took a step nearer, brandishing his safety razor in righteous indignation.

"It's a shame, I tell you. You don't seem to have any conscience or any sense of proportion. You'd flirt with a cigar-Indian if there wasn't anything else around. Why can't you leave these young people alone? Do you think I like the idea of your spending the evening here snug and warm with that Frenchman while I'm shuttling around with that silly girl in the dark?"

"Mortimer, you're ungallant! What has poor Aurora ever done to you?" She turned in her chair, looked at him, and then burst into laughter. He watched her with a puzzled frown. He never knew exactly how to take *Patricia* when she laughed at him.

"If you only knew how funny you look, Mort, dear. There's a smudge of soap on the end of your nose and you look like a charlotte russe." She rose slowly, put her fingers on his arm, and looked up into his eyes with a very winning expression.

"Don't be silly, dear," she said, softly. "You know you said you weren't going to doubt me again—ever. I know what I'm about. I have a duty, a sacred duty to perform and you're going to take your share of it."

"A duty?"

She nodded. "You're not to know until it's all over. You mustn't question, you're to be good and do exactly what I tell you to do. Won't you, Mort? *There*, I knew you would. It's such a little thing to do."

She leaned as close to him as she could without getting soap on her face.

"I'll tell you a secret if you'll promise to be nice. I don't like the man—really I don't—not at all."

He looked in her eyes and believed her. "You always get your way in the end, don't you?" he said, after a pause.

"Of course I do. What would be the *use* of a way, if one didn't *have* it?"

That seemed unanswerable logic, so Crabb grinned.

"You're a queer one, *Patty*," which, as Patricia knew, meant that she was the most extraordinary and wonderful of persons. So she smiled at the back of his head as he went out because she agreed with him.

CHAPTER XVIII

PATRICIA'S dinner drew to its delectable close, and coffee had already been served when the butler went to the front door and brought back a telegram on a silver tray.

Patricia picked it up and turned it over daintily.

"For you, Aurora," she said.

Aurora with apologies tore open the envelope and read, her brow clouding.

"I hope it's nothing serious," said Patricia, sweetly sympathetic.

Aurora rose hurriedly. "I don't know," she said dubiously, and then reading: " 'Aunt Jane sick, motor over this evening if possible.' There's no signature. I suppose I'll have to go." Her lip protruded childishly. "How tiresome!"

"It's very inconsiderate of her, isn't it?"

said *Patricia*. The look of incomprehension still lingered on the young girl's face.

"I can't see what she wants of me," she murmured.

"Perhaps she's seriously ill," *Patricia* volunteered.

"Perhaps—yes, I must go, of course. But how can I?"

"Mortimer," *Patricia* provided the cue.

"I'll drive you, Aurora," said Crabb.

"And Louis?"

DeLaunay made no sign.

"I will take care of the Monsieur DeLaunay, dear. Do you think you could trust me?"

Aurora's lips said, "Of course," but her eyes winked rapidly several times as she adapted her mind to the situation.

The decision reached, DeLaunay stepped forward.

"If you wish that I should go——"

"Quite unnecessary," put in *Patricia*, quickly. "If your aunt Jane is sick, Aurora——"

208

Aurora hung in the wind a regretful moment.

"Oh, yes—he'd be in the way. I'll leave him with you, *Patty*. *Please* don't flirt any more than you can help."

"My dear child," said *Patty*, with solemn conviction, "since poor, foolish Freddy Winthrop, engaged men are *taboo*. Besides, tonight I have other plans. I would not flirt if you could animate the Apollo Belvedere. As Mortimer so chastely puts it, 'me for the downy at 10 G. M.' Monsieur will doubtless practice pool-shots or play a game of *N*apoleon."

"Oh, yes," said the Frenchman, with a calmness which scarcely concealed the note of derision.

But Aurora, after one long look in his direction, had vanished to don motor clothing, and when she came down, Mortimer Crabb with his quivering car awaited her in the drive. *Patricia* and the Baron waved them good-by from the porch and then went

indoors to the subtle effulgence of the drawing room. *Patricia* walked to the mantel,
turned her back to the fire and stretched her
shapely arms along its shelf, facing her guest
with level gaze and a smile which was something between a taunt and a caress. DeLaunay
inhaled luxiously the smoke of his cigarette
and appraised his hostess through the half-
closed eyes of the artist searching for a "mo-
tif." She was puzzling—this woman—like
the vagrant color in a landscape in the afternoon sunlight, which shimmered one moment
in the sun and in the next was lost in
shadowy mystery—not the mystery of the
solemn hills, but the playful mystery of the
woodland brook which laughs mockingly
from secret places. Her eyes were laughing at him. He felt it, though none of the
physical symbols of laughter were offered in
evidence.

"I'm so sorry, Monsieur," she began in
French. "It is *such* a pity. There is no excuse for any one to have a sick aunt when the

stage is set for sentiment. I had planned your evening so carefully, too——"

"You are the soul of kindness, Madame," he said politely, still studying her.

"Yes," she went on, slowly, "I think I am. But then I am *chez moi,* and charity, you know, begins at home."

"I hope you will not call it charity. Charity they say is cold. And you, Madame, whatever you would seek to express, are not cold."

"How can you know?"

"Your eyes——"

"My *beaux yeux* again." She shrugged her shoulders, and turned toward the door. "It is time, I think, for you to practice pool-shots."

"Ah, you are cruel!" He stepped before her and held out protesting hands. "I do not care for pool, Madame."

"Or Napoleon?"

"No—I wish to talk with you. *Please!*"

She paused, appraising him sideways.

"I have some letters to write," she said, briefly.

"*Please*, Madame." He stood before her, his slender figure gracefully bent, motioning appealingly toward the deep davenport, which was set invitingly in front of the fire. She followed his gesture with her eyes, then with a light laugh passed before him and sat down.

"*N*othing about my *beaux yeux* then," she mocked.

He glanced at her with a smile which showed his fine teeth and sank beside her and at a distance.

"*Voilà*, Madame! You see? I am an angel of discretion."

She smiled approvingly. "I'm glad we understand each other."

"Do we?" he asked with a suggestion of effrontery.

"I hope so."

"I'm not so sure. To me you are still a mystery."

"Am I? *That's* curious. I've tried to make my meaning plain. *Perhaps* I can make it clearer. For some weeks you have been making love to me, Monsieur. I don't like it. I never flirt, except with the very ancient or the very youthful," she said mendaciously. "You don't come within my age limits."

He laughed gayly.

"Love is of all ages and no ages. I am both ancient and youthful. Old in hope, young in despair—in affairs of the heart, I assure you, a veritable babe in the arms. I have never really loved—until now."

"Why do you marry Aurora then?" she put in.

He looked at her with a puzzled brow, then laughed merrily. "Madame, you are too clever to waste your time in America." But as *Patricia* was looking very gravely into the fire, he too relapsed into silence, and frowned at the ash of his cigarette.

"I do not see, Madame, why we should speak of her," he said, sulkily. "It must be clear to you that our understanding is complete. The marriages in my country, as you know——"

"Oh, yes, I know," she interrupted, "but Miss *N*orth is different. She has not the social ambitions of other girls. Miss *N*orth is romantic but quite unspoiled. Has it occurred to you that pérhaps she may hope for a somewhat different relation between you?"

"We are good friends—very good friends. She is enchanting," he said with enthusiasm, "so innocent of the ways of the world, so talented, so charming. We shall be very happy."

"I hope so," dryly.

He examined her shrewdly.

"You have her happiness close to your heart! Is it not so? What is to be feared? I shall be very good to her. We understand each other. She will be glad of the splendor of my ancient name, and I desire the means to restore my estates and place myself in a position of influence among my people. I care for her as one cares for a lovely flower—but the mind—the soul, Madame, I have found them —elsewhere," he leaned forward and touched her fingers with his own.

Patricia's gaze was far away. It seemed as though she was unconscious of his touch. "It is a pity," she said, softly, "a great pity. I am very sorry."

"Could you not learn to care a little?"

She turned on him then, but her voice was still gentle.

"We are not in France, Monsieur," she said coldly.

"What does that matter?" he urged. "Love knows nothing of geography. Love is a cosmopolite. It cares not for time or place or convention. I care for you very much, Madame, and whatever you may think, it makes me happy to tell you so."

"And Aurora?" *Patricia* reiterated the word, like the clanging of an alarm bell.

The Baron relaxed his grasp and lowered his head.

She leaned forward, elbow on knee, looking into the fire.

"You know, Baron, I'm very sorry for Aurora."

As he made no comment she went on:

"She has always been a very sweet, amiable, honorable child. I'm very fond of her. She was very much alone with her books and her family. She has always lived in an atmosphere of her own—an atmosphere that she made for herself, without companions of her own age. Her mother brought her up without the slightest knowledge of the guile, the deceit, or wickedness of the world in which some day she was to live. They used even to scan the newspapers before she was permitted to read them, and clip out objectionable paragraphs. Even I have done that since she has been here visiting me. Her father was always too busy making money to bother. At the age of twenty she is still a dreamer, old in nothing but years, living in an idyl of her own, the sleeping princess in the fairy-tale whom you,

216

the gallant prince, have awakened with a kiss."

DeLaunay's shoulders moved slightly as he sighed.

"*T*hat kiss, Monsieur! You have awakened her," she went on, "to what?" She paused abruptly and turned toward him for a reply.

"Your question is hardly flattering to my vanity," he said, smiling. "*T*here are women———"

"She is a child."

"All women are children. I shall find means to make her happy."

*P*atricia resumed her study of the fire.

"I hope so. With money your opportunities for happiness would be greater. Without money———" she paused and shook her head slowly.

The Baron turned abruptly, but *P*atricia's gaze was fixed upon the fire. When he spoke his tones were suppressed—his manner constrained.

"Madame—what do you mean?"

She faced him slowly, her expression gently sympathetic.

"Have you not heard?"

"Heard what, Madame?"

"Of Monsieur *North's* misfortune—you must have seen it in the newspapers——"

"The newspapers! *No*—what is it?"

"Monsieur *North* has lost his money."

DeLaunay rose quickly, one hand before him as though to ward off a blow.

"What you tell me is impossible," he said thickly.

"*No*," gravely. "It is true."

He stared at her unbelieving, but her eyes met his calmly, eagerly, and in their depths he saw only pity.

"Would I not have heard this dreadful thing, Madame? Aurora would have told me."

"She might have told you if she had known."

"She did not know?"

"*T*hey want to save her the pain. *T*hey always have. *T*hat is one reason why she is stopping here with me. Don't you understand?"

DeLaunay showed other signs of inquietude and was now pacing the rug nervously.

"It is incredible!" he was saying, "incredible! I cannot—no——" And he stopped before her. "*No*, I will not believe it!"

Patricia clasped her hands over her knees and was looking very gravely into the fire. She had the air of a person who is mourning the loss of a very dear friend.

"How do you know this?" he asked again, anxiously.

"From Mrs. *North* a week ago, when she let Aurora come to me. But it is no secret now, as it has been in the newspapers. I have kept them from Aurora. She is so happy here with you—I hadn't the heart to do anything to destroy her pleasure."

"But *North* and Company is a very great business house. So rich that even in France we have heard of them."

"Yes—Mr. North has been rich for years,"

and then with a sigh, "It is very sad—very, very sad."

"But how could such a thing happen? Surely he is wise enough——"

"Speculation!" said *Patricia*, simply. "All of our business men speculate. Even the oldest—the wisest."

DeLaunay sank into a chair at some distance, his head in his hands. *"Dieu!"* she heard him mutter. "What a terrible country. I cannot believe——"

Patricia got up at last and walked over and put her hand quietly on his shoulder. She was even smiling.

"I am so sorry, Monsieur. Of course you know that, don't you? But I am sure everything will turn out for the best. Aurora loves you. You must remember that poverty will make no difference in the relations between you. She will even welcome the chance to be poor—she wants to be of some real use in the world—she has said so—you had even planned that, Monsieur!"

220

The Frenchman turned just one look in her direction, a look in which despair, inquietude, inquiry and anger were curiously blended and then rose and strode the length of the room away.

"You are mocking me. You know, Madame —that—that it is impossible—this marriage— if—what you tell me is true."

"I wish I could reassure you," slowly.

"What proofs have you?"

"Isn't my word enough?"

"Yes, but——"

"You want confirmation. Very well!" Patricia walked to the library table, opened its drawer, and took out the *Sun* and *Herald*. As she opened them two paper cuttings and a pair of scissors fell to the floor. She picked them up before DeLaunay could reach her, opening the newspapers, both of which bore signs of mutilation. And while he wondered what she was about to do or say, she resumed calmly, even indifferently. "I had clipped these papers that Aurora might not see them.

Since you profess some incredulity, perhaps you'd rather read for yourself." And she handed them to him.

He adjusted his monocle with trembling fingers, and began reading the slips, his lips moving, his eyes dilated, while *Patricia* watched him, her eyes masked by her fingers. She saw him read one article through, then scan the other, his lips compressed, his small chin working forward.

"Five million dollars!" he whispered at last. "It is terrible—terrible. And there will be nothing at all."

"It looks so, doesn't it?" she replied. "Read on."

And he read the remainder of it aloud, pausing at each sentence as though fascinated by the horror of it. When he had read the last word, the papers dropped from his fingers upon the tea-table beside him. At a grimace his eye-glass dropped the length of its cord and he stood erect, squaring his shoulders and straightening to his small height with the air of a man who has made a resolution.

"Madame," he said, more calmly, "this is very disagreeable news."

"It's quite sad, isn't it? But I must warn you against speaking to Aurora just yet. The news is spreading fast enough and to-morrow it may be necessary to tell her. In the meanwhile you must be gentle with her and tender—you can comfort her so much. She will need all your kindness now, Monsieur."

But DeLaunay had taken out his watch. "Madame, I thank you for your kindness to me, but I am—I am much perturbed—I—I do not want to see Miss North until I can think what I must do. Would you mind if I went in town to my hotel——"

"To-night?"

"Yes—to-night."

"She will think it strange for you to go without a word."

"I—I——"

"You could leave a note."

"You will permit me?"

Patricia watched him seat himself heavily at her writing-desk.

"Monsieur," she asked, "what will you say to her?"

"That I am ill—that I——"

"How will that help either you or her?"

He shrugged his shoulders hopelessly.

"What then, Madame?"

"I don't know," she said, slowly. "It is a very painful note to write. I am very sorry for you, sorry for Miss North, sorry for myself that you learned of this through me. It is curious that no one told you," she sighed. "But perhaps it is just as well that you know."

"I am grateful, Madame, I cannot tell you how grateful," he began, but she held up her hand.

"It pains me to see Miss North unhappy, but I know more of life than she does. I was educated in France, Monsieur, and I know what is expected of American girls who marry into the *ancienne noblesse*—the *noblesse de souche.* Of course, without a *dot,* this marriage is impossible."

"Yes, Madame, that is true. It is—impossible, absolutely impossible."

"Aurora—Miss North believes in your love for her—she will hardly understand——"

DeLaunay swung around in his chair and rose, facing the hostess.

"There must be no misunderstanding between us," decisively, "I shall go at once."

"That's your decision—your final decision?"

"It is—final."

By this time she stood beside him at the desk, and as she spoke her finger pointed to the paper and ink.

"Then you must write her to-night—before you go. It would not be fair to leave matters to me. It is not fair to her or to yourself. Sit down, Monsieur, and write."

He sank into the chair again.

"And what shall I write?"

"If I can help you——" sweetly.

"I will write what you say," with a sigh of relief.

So *Patricia* seated herself beside him and with a troubled brow dictated in English.

"My dear Miss *North:*

"I have learned with horror and dismay of the great bereavement which has fallen upon you and your family, but in view of this misfortune, I have thought it wisest to take my departure at once.

"You will understand, of course, that under these conditions it is advisable to discontinue our present relations at once, and as my presence might prove embarrassing I leave with feelings of great unhappiness. You are doubtless aware of the customs of my country in the matter of settlements, the absence of which would preclude the possibility of marriage on my part.

"Mrs. Crabb has kindly consented to make my apologies and excuses to you for my abrupt departure which I take with deep regret, the deeper because of my profound esteem for your many delightful qualities, of which you may be assured I shall never cease to think with tender and regretful sentiments——"

Patricia broke off abruptly. "I think that is all, Monsieur. Will you finish it—as you please?"

The baron nodded and added:

"I am, Mademoiselle, with profound assurances of my friendship and consideration,

"Yours,

"Louis Charles Bertram de Chartres,

"Baron DeLaunay."

Patricia meanwhile had ordered the Baron's suitcase packed and had 'phoned for a station wagon and a while later stood in the hallway speeding the parting guest.

"Must you go, Monsieur? I am so very sorry. I understand, of course. I am the loser." And with all the generosity of a victorious general whose enemy is no longer dangerous. "If you are nice you may kiss my hand."

As DeLaunay bent over her fingers he murmured: "If it had only been *you,* Madame."

And in a moment he had gone.

CHAPTER XIX

PATRICIA stood in the hallway a moment looking at the note to Aurora, which she held in her fingers. Then she went to the desk so recently vacated by her guest and wrote steadily for an hour. Her thesis was the international marriage, and she called it Crabb vs. DeLaunay, enclosing two papers, DeLaunay's note and the newspaper clippings from her adorable printers. Slips of paper were pinned to them, upon one of which she had written "Exhibit A," and on the other "Exhibit B." She sealed them all in a long envelope addressed to Miss North and handed it to Aurora's maid with instructions that it should be given to her mistress when she had gone up to her room.

From her own bed Patricia heard the motor arrive and her husband fuming in the hallway below, the sound of Aurora's door closing and of Mortimer's heavy footsteps in his own quarters; then after awhile, silence. She lay on her bed in the dark thinking, listening intently. It was long before she was rewarded. Then her door opened quietly, and in the aperture the night-lamp showed a pale, tear-stained face and a slender, girlish figure swathed in a pale blue dressing gown.

"*Patricia!*" the girl half sobbed, half whispered, "*Patty!*"

Patricia rose in her bed and took the slender figure into her sheltering arms. "Aurora —darling. I've been waiting for you. Can you forgive me?"

"Yes—yes," sobbed the girl. "I understand."

"You were too good for him, Aurora, dear. He wasn't worthy of you." And then, as an afterthought. "But then, I don't know a man who is."

Patricia breathed a sigh of relief. She had thought it was going to be more difficult. She made room for the girl in the bed beside her and soothed and petted her until she fell asleep.

"*Poor Aurora,*" she murmured softly to herself. "You were never destined for a life like that, child. The man you marry is to be an American, a fine, young, healthy animal like yourself. I will not tell you his name because if I did, you'd probably refuse him, and of course that would never do. It must be managed some way. He's poor, you know, dear, but then that won't matter because you will have enough for both."

It did not take Aurora a great while to recover from the shock of disillusion and before long she was out on the golf links again, with her usual happy following. Aurora had many virtues as well as accomplishments, and *Patricia* was very fond of her. During the winter in the city, she had given a dinner for her to which Stephen Ventnor was invited. *Patricia's* plan had succeeded admirably, for Ventnor, after several years of indomitable faithfulness to the ashes of the mourned Pa-

tricia, had suddenly come to life. He liked
Aurora so much that he didn't even take the
trouble to hide his new emotion from *Patricia.*
Patricia sighed, for even now renunciation
was difficult to her, but when she moved into
the country for the summer, she held out the
latch-string to him for the week ends so
that he could come out every week and play
golf with Aurora, which showed that
after all marriage had taught *Patricia* something.

Patricia had decided that Aurora *North*
was to marry Steve Ventnor, and this resolution made she left no stone unturned to bring
the happy event to a consummation. The skil-
ful maker of opportunities she remembered
sometimes trusted to opportunity to make itself. *Propinquity*, she knew, was her first lieutenant and the unobtrusive way in which these
two young people were continually thrown together must have been a surprise even to themselves. Ventnor took his two weeks of vacation in July and spent them at the Crabbs'.

Patricia had thought that those two weeks would have brought the happy business to a conclusion—for Aurora was just ready to be caught on the rebound, and Ventnor was now very much in love. But when Steve's vacation was over and he had packed his trunk to go mournfully back to town, *Patricia* knew that something had happened to change her well-laid plans.

She had never given Jimmy McLemore a thought. She had seen the three many times during the summer from her bedroom windows, Aurora, Steve and McLemore, but the thought of Aurora having a tenderness for the golfing automaton had never for a moment entered her mind. She watched Mr. Ventnor's departing back with mingled feelings.

"You'll be out on Saturday as usual, won't you, Steve?" she asked.

"Oh, yes, thank you, *Patty*," he replied, "I'll be out, if you'll have me. But there isn't much use, you know."

"Don't be so meek, Steve!" she cried.

"You're impossible when you're that way. What earthly use did you make of all of my training?"

Ventnor smiled mournfully.

"You didn't begin soon enough, *Patty*," he said.

That pleased *Patricia* and she made a mental resolution that marry Aurora, Steve should, if it lay in her power to accomplish it.

"*T*here's something wrong with that girl," she mused, as she watched Aurora and "the Sphynx"—as McLemore was familiarly called—playing the fifth hole. "Anybody who can see anything marriageable in Jimmy McLemore, ought to be carefully confined behind a garden wall. Jimmy! I would as soon think of marrying a statue of Buddha."

The *Blue Wing* was out of commission for the summer. Mortimer insisted that no sane man could maintain both a big yacht and a big country place. But *Patricia* was very happy and watched the development of Steve Ventnor's romance with a jealous eye. She was obliged to admit, as the summer lengthened into autumn, that after all, the whole thing was very much a matter of golf.

Aurora was golf mad, Patricia knew, and when Jimmy McLemore ran down a twenty-foot putt for a "bird" on the sixteenth hole, thereby winning "three up and two" from Steve Ventnor, the golf championship of the Country Club, Patricia detached herself from the "gallery" which had followed the players and made her way sadly to the Club House veranda. Penelope Wharton, her sister, who was fond of Ventnor, followed, the picture of dejection. In the morning round Steve had been "one up"; and the hopes of the two women had run high that their champion would be able to increase his lead during the afternoon, or at least to maintain it against his redoubtable adversary, but after the first few holes the victor had developed one of those "streaks" for which he was famous, and though poor old Steve had played a steady up-hill game, the luck went against him and he knew at the tenth hole that unless McLemore fell over in a fit, the gold cup was lost—for that year at least.

Patricia realized, too, that the famous gold cup might not be the only prize at stake.

"And now," she said wrathfully, "she'll probably marry that *person*." Mr. McLemore would have withered could he have seen the expression in *Patricia's* eyes, for when *Patricia* called any human being a "person," it meant that her thoughts were unutterable.

"I suppose so," said *Penelope*.

"I've no patience with Aurora *N*orth," said *Patty*, "she's absolutely lacking in a sense of proportion. Imagine letting one's life happiness hang on the fate of a single putt."

"And Steve is *such* a dear."

"He is, that's the worst of it—and they're eminently fitted for each other in every way—by birth, breeding, and circumstances. As a sportsman *J*immy may be a success, but as a gentleman—as a lover—as a *husband*——"

16

Patricia's two brown hands were raised in protest toward Olympus. "It's odious, Pen, a case for a grand jury—or a coroner!"

"Aurora is too nice a girl," sighed *Pene*-lope.

"*Nice!* In everything but discrimination. That's the peril of being an 'out-of-door girl.' The more muscle, the less gray matter. That kind of thing disturbs the balance of power." Patricia sighed—"Oh, I tried it and I know. A woman with too much muscle is like an over-rigged yawl—all right in light airs, but dangerous in a blow. What's the use? Our greatest strength after all, is weakness."

"I'm sure you couldn't convince Aurora of that—nor Steve."

"I don't know," said *Patricia*, slowly, "but I'd like to try."

Further talk was interrupted by the arrival of the crowd from the fair-green, thirsty and controversial. Steve Ventnor, like the good loser that he was, had been the first to shake McLemore by the hand in congratulation, and

236

if he was heavy of heart, his smiling face gave no sign of it. For the present, at least, he had abandoned the field to his conqueror who brought up the rear of the "gallery" with Aurora, accepting handshakes right and left with the changeless dignity which had gained him his sobriquet of "Sphynx." At the veranda steps Mortimer Crabb took him in tow and brought him to the table where *Penelope* and *Patricia* were mournfully absorbing lemonade.

"Too bad, Steve," said *Patricia* with a brightness that failed to deceive. "*N*obody with mere blood in his veins can expect to compete with a hydraulic ram. He's a wonderful piece of mechanism—Jimmy is—but I'm always tortured with the fear that he may forget to wind himself up some morning. Mort, couldn't you have dropped a little sand in his bearings?"

"Oh, he's got plenty of sand," said Crabb generously.

"He's a cracking good golfer," said Steve,

looking reprovingly at *Patricia*. "He's the better man, that's all."

He sank beside *Patricia* while Crabb had a steward take the orders.

"No," muttered *Patricia*. "Not that, not the better man, only the better golfer, Steve." And then with a sudden and mystifying change of manner, "Do you know why he always wears a crimson vest?"

"No—I've never thought," replied Steve.

"It's very—un—er—unprofessional—isn't it?"

"It isn't what a man wears that wins holes, you know, *Patty*."

"Oh, no," she said, carelessly, "I was just wondering——"

Mortimer Crabb, unofficial host of the occasion, had beckoned to Aurora and McLemore, who now joined the party. Steve Ventnor rose as the girl approached and their eyes met. Aurora's eyes were the color of lapis-lazuli, but the deep tan of her skin made them seem several shades lighter. They were handsome eyes, very clear and expressive, and at important moments like the present ones her long lashes effectually screened what might have been read in their depths.

"I'm sorry, Steve," she said gently. "You didn't have enough practice."

"Are you really?" asked Steve. He bent his head forward and said something for Aurora's ears alone, at which her lids dropped still further and the ends of her lips curved demurely. But she did not reply, and turned in evident relief when Crabb made a hospitable suggestion.

Patricia watched the by-play with interest. She had followed the romance with mingled feelings, for it was apparent that the triangle which had been equilateral in the spring was now distorted out of all semblance to its former shape, with poor Steve getting the worst of it. The reason was clear. The Sphynx was rich and so could afford to play golf with Aurora every day of the year if he wished, while Steve Ventnor, who spent his daylight hours selling bonds in the city, had to make the most of his Saturday and Sunday afternoons. It was really too bad.

But the Sphynx only smiled his unhumorous smile, and went on playing golf during the week when Ventnor was at work. Propinquity had done a damage which even Patricia, with all her worldliness, could not find available means to repair. But she joined good-humoredly in the toasts to the new club champion who was accepting his honors carelessly, keeping her eyes meanwhile on Jimmy McLemore's crimson vest. That vest was a part of Jimmy's golf, as much a part of it as his tauric glasses, his preliminary wiggle on the tee, or his maddening precision on the putting-green. It fascinated her somehow, almost to the exclusion of the gayety in which she rightfully had a part.

The gold cup was brought forth and passed from hand to hand. As it came to *Patricia* she looked at it inside and out, read the inscription leisurely, then handed it carelessly to her neighbor.

"Chaste and quite expensive," was her comment.

"Oh, I think it's beautiful," said Aurora, reprovingly.

"Chaque enfant à son gou gou, my dear," said *Patricia.* "You know, Aurora, I never did approve of golf prizes—especially valuable ones. After all, golf is merely a game—not a religion. It's the habit in this club to consider a golf cup with the same kind of an eye that one gives to a possible seat in *Paradise.*"

Even Steve Ventnor thought *Patricia's* remarks in bad taste.

"If Jimmy plays the game of life the way he played golf to-day," he laughed, "he'll have an eighteen-karat halo, and no mistake."

"Patty!" exclaimed Miss *North,* reprovingly. "You know you don't believe a word you say. You love golf prizes. Why you're always giving the Bachelors' Cup, and this

year you've presented the cup for the 'Affinity Foursomes.' Besides, you've won at least three prizes yourself."

"I've reformed," said *Patricia*, decisively. "I've lost patience with golf. I haven't any interest in a game that requires the elimination of all human attributes."

"What on earth are you talking about?"

"One can't be entirely human and play a good game of golf, that's all," she announced.

"*That's* rough on McLemore," laughed Mortimer.

"It's human to be irritated, human to be angry, human to have nerves, human to make mistakes. I've no patience with people who can't lose their tempers."

"I'm apt to lose mine, if you keep calling me names," said the Sphynx, affably.

"You couldn't, Jimmy," said *Patricia*, soberly. "Anyone who can make the tenth, eleventh and twelfth in eleven playing out of two bunkers will never lose his temper in this

242

world—or anything else," she added, *sotto voce.*

"There won't be any more Bachelors' Cups, then?"

"Not if I can help it. At least not for the Ancient and Honorable Game as we play it now. The Bachelors' Cup this fall will be played for across country." The members of the party examined her as though they believed she had suddenly been bereft of her senses—all but her husband, who knew that in being surprised at Patty, one was wasting valuable energy, but even Mortimer was mildly curious.

"Across country!" they asked.

"Exactly. I'm going to invest the game with a real sporting interest, develop the possibilities of the niblick, eliminate the merely mechanical, introduce a stronger element of chance. The course will be laid out like a 'drag.'"

"With an anise-seed bag?" queried Crabb.

Patricia withered her husband with a look.

"With scraps of paper," she asserted, firmly. "The course will be four miles long over good hunting country."

"You can't mean it," said McLemore.

"I do. It's quite feasible."

"Yes, but——"

"It's a good sporting proposition," said Aurora North, suddenly kindling to interest. "Why not?"

Ventnor and McLemore only smiled amusedly, as became true golfers.

"Oh you can laugh, you two. Why not give it a trial? Just to make it interesting I'll offer a cup for the Club champion and runner-up. It will be a pretty cup—and Aurora and I will caddy."

"Willingly," laughed Aurora.

There the matter stopped. It was a joke, of course, and both men realized it, but any joke in which Aurora North had a part was the joke for them. A week passed before Patricia completed her plans and in the meanwhile everybody had forgotten all about her

244

amazing proposition. It was, therefore, with surprise and not a little amusement that Mc-Lemore and Ventnor received the dainty notice in *Patricia's* handwriting, which advised them that the Cross Country Match would be played off on the following Thursday afternoon, at two o'clock. Jimmy McLemore smiled at a photograph on the desk in his library, but later in the day after a talk over the telephone with Aurora he got a mashie, and a heavy mid-iron from his bag and went out in his own cow-pasture to practice. Steve Ventnor in his office in the city turned the note over in his fingers and frowned. *Thurs*day was his busiest day, but he realized that he had given his promise and that if McLemore played he must. It was a very silly business. Several things mystified him, however. What did *Patricia* mean, for instance, by the absurd lines at the bottom of his invitation? "Aurora will caddy for you; and don't wear a crimson vest—there's nothing to be gained by it."

On a slip of paper enclosed were the *local rules:*

(1) The first ball and every fourth ball there-after may be played from a rubber tee.

(2) A ball in "casual" water may be lifted and dropped without penalty.

(3) Running brooks, ponds, rocks, fences, etc., are natural hazards, and must be played over as such.

(4) A lost ball means the loss of one stroke, but not of distance. A ball may be dropped within twenty-five yards of the spot where ball disappeared.

(5) *The match must be finished* within four hours. The competitor who for any reason fails to finish loses the match.

Steve Ventnor smiled as he read, but in spite of his golf sense, which is like no other sense in the world, felt himself gently warming to the project. He would go of course— for Aurora was to caddy for him.

CHAPTER XX

EVEN Mortimer Crabb was excluded from that charming luncheon of four. It was very informal and great was the merriment at Patricia's expense, but through it all she smiled calmly at their scepticism—as Columbus at Salamanca must have smiled, if he ever did, or Newton or Edison, or any others of the world's great innovators.

"Cross-country golf," she continued proudly to assert, "is the golf of the New Era."

"Do you really mean it, Patty?" asked Aurora seriously, when the men had gone upstairs to change.

"Of course I do, Aurora. The Ancient and Honorable Game has its limitations. Cross-country golf has none. You'll see, my dear, in ten years, they'll be playing distance matches between New York and Philadelphia

—the fewest strokes in the shortest time—that *will* be a game."

"And who'll pay for the lost balls?" asked Aurora, laughing.

"*That*, Aurora," replied *Patricia* with a touch of dignity, "is something with which I am remotely concerned."

The men came down stairs dressed for the fray, grinning broadly, and *Patricia*, after a glance at McLemore's red vest, took up his golf bag with a business-like air and led the way to the terrace. The Sphynx blinked through his tauric glasses at her unresponsive back silhouetted in the doorway, but as Aurora had taken Steve's bag, he followed meekly, submitting to the inevitable. Outside, *Patricia* was indicating a rift in the row of maples which bordered her vegetable garden, through which was to be seen the brown sweep of the meadow beyond.

"The drive is through there. You'll get the direction marks for your second. The dis-

248

tance is four miles. The finish is on Aurora's lawn—the putting-green near the rear portico of the house. Drive off, gentlemen."

The honor was Mr. McLemore's. With a saddish smile, half of pity and half of a protest for his outraged golfing dignity, he took his bag from *Patricia*, and with a frugality which did him credit, upturned the bag on the lawn, spilling out a miscellany of old balls which he had saved for practice strokes. Selecting half a dozen, he stuffed five of them in his pockets, returned the newer ones to his bag and scorning the rubber tee which Patricia offered him, dropped a ball over his shoulder and took his cleek out of his bag. Each act was sportsman-like—a fine expression of the golfing spirit.

The drive went straight—and they saw it bouncing coquettishly up the meadow beyond. Steve, with the munificence which only poverty knows, brought forth a new ball, took the rubber tee and, with his driver, got off a long low one which cleared the bushes and vanished over the brow of the hill.

"A new golfing era has begun," said Patricia, with the air of a prophet.

"If I ever find my ball," said Ventnor, dubiously.

"What do you care, Steve, as long as you're making history?" laughed Aurora, with a sly glance at their hostess.

Patricia, unperturbed, led the way through a breach in the hedge and out into the sunlight where she raised a crimson parasol, which no one had noticed before.

"My complexion," she explained to Aurora. "One can't be too careful when one gets to be —ahem—thirty.   Besides, it just matches Jimmy's vest."

The grass in the pasture was short and Mc-Lemore played his brassey—his caddy instructing him as to the ground on the other side, which fell gently down to a brook he could not reach.

"I got that one away," said McLemore, livening to his task. "It's not really bad going at all."

Patricia smiled gratefully, but made no response, for Steve, a little further on, was in a hole and had to play out with a mashie, which he did with consummate skill, the ball rolling down the hill thirty yards short of McLemore's.

From the hilltop they could easily see the line of the paper chase which *Patricia* had laid when she rode over the course yesterday. It stretched across the lower end of the Renwick's meadows along the road, crossing two streams, bordered with willow trees and led straight for Waterman's stone quarry. Ventnor played a careful mid-iron which cleared the brook and bounded forward into the meadow beyond; but McLemore overreached himself trying for distance and found the brook, losing his ball and two strokes; but he teed up, having played five and lay six well down the meadow, within carrying distance of the second stream. But

Steve, playing steadily, passed him with his fourth, a long cleek shot which fell just short of the stream.

Beyond the creek was the hill to the quarry, three shots for McLemore, two long ones for Ventnor. With excellent judgment McLemore played safely over the creek with a mid-iron, reaching the brink of the quarry in two more, which gave him a chance to tee up on his ninth for the long drive across. Steve Ventnor was less fortunate, dribbling his sixth up the hill, fifty yards short of the quarry, into which, trying a long cleek shot to clear it, he unfortunately drove. He waited to see the Sphynx carefully tee his ball and send it straight down the course which *Patricia* indicated, and then taking the bag from his caddy helped her into the path which zigzagged down to where his ball lay, a hundred feet below.

Patricia and the Sphynx had chosen the shorter way through the woods at the upper end and Steve and Aurora were alone.

At the bottom of the slope behind a projecting crag Steve stopped and faced his companion.

"Aurora," he said.

"Yes, Steve."

"Is it true you're going to marry McLemore?"

Aurora picked a flower which grew in a ledge beside her before she replied.

"Why do you ask?"

"I thought I'd like to know, that's all. People say you are——"

"I haven't said so."

"*Then,*" eagerly, "you aren't?"

"I don't see what right you've got to ask."

"I haven't—only I thought I'd like to be the first to congratulate him."

"Oh, is that all?"

"And I thought I'd like to tell you again that I love you better than anybody could—and that I always will, even if you marry him. He's a very nice fellow but—but I'll be very unhappy——"

"Will you? I don't believe it."

"Why do you say that?"

"Because you're too cool about it. You wouldn't think he was such a nice fellow if you were jealous of him. Why haven't you played more with me this summer?"

"I had to work—you know that. What's the use——"

"If you love me as you say you do, I don't see how you could be so cool about—about seeing us together——"

"Perhaps I wasn't as cool as I looked. See here, Aurora, you mustn't talk like that." He had turned and before she could escape him, had taken her in his arms and was kissing her. "Don't say I'm cool. I love you, Aurora, with every ounce that's in me. I want you more than I can ever want anything again in this world or the next. I'm not going to let you marry that fellow or anybody else—do you understand?"

She had yielded for a moment to his warmth because there didn't seem to be anything else to do. But when she slowly disengaged herself from his arms and faced him her eyes were wet and the color flamed through her tan.

"Steve!" she stammered. "Steve!—how could you?"

But he still faced her passionately, undaunted. "It's true," he said huskily. "I love you—you can't marry him—I won't let you——"

He took a step forward but this time she retreated.

"Don't, Steve—not again—not now—you mustn't. They'll be coming out in the open there in a moment. I'll never say you are cool again—never—after that. You're not cool—not in the least—I was mistaken. I've never seen you—like this before—you're different——"

"You made me do it. I couldn't stand your saying I didn't care. I'm not sorry," he went on, "he couldn't love you the way I do."

"I think perhaps you're right," said Aurora coolly. "In the meantime——"

"Won't you give me an answer?"

"In the meanwhile," she went on, preening her disordered hair, "you are supposed to be playing the golf of the *N*ew Era——"

"Aurora——"

"*N*o," she had taken up his golf bag and was walking away.

"Won't you answer me?" he pleaded

"Get your ball out of this quarry," she said, relentlessly, "and I'll think about it."

It took Steve Ventnor thirteen strokes to play out of that quarry, which, for a fellow with a record of seventy-two at Apawomeck, was "going it." The first stroke he missed clean; the second he sliced into a clay-bank; his third struck the rocks and bounded back against the wall behind him, finding lodgment at last in some bushes where he took three more. To make matters worse, Aurora was laughing at him, hysterically, unrestrainedly, and *P*atricia and the Sphynx, who had ap-

"'You are supposed to be playing the golf of the New Era.'"

peared on the path above, were joining in the merriment.

"Oh, I'll lift," he growled at last.

"You can't," laughed Aurora. "It's against the rules." And Patricia appealed to, confirmed the statement.

Three more swings he took, each of them in impossible lies, the last of which smashed his niblick. After that there followed a period of strange calmness—of desperation, while he worked his ball into a good lie on the far side of the quarry from which, with a fine mashie shot he lifted it over the cliffs and into the open beyond.

Steve Ventnor toiled wearily up the hill at the heels of his caddy, struggling for his lost composure. He caught up with Aurora at a point half-way up where he took the golf bag from her shoulder and faced her again.

"Won't you answer me, Aurora?" he pleaded, breathlessly.

"No, I won't," she said, calmly. "You swore—horribly—in the bushes."

"I didn't."

"I heard you," firmly. "I'll never marry a man who swears," and she hurried on. When Ventnor joined the others, he found Patricia sitting on a rock making up the score, which at the present moment stood: Ventnor —20; McLemore—9.

"How do you like it, Steve?" asked Patricia, still figuring.

"Oh, it's great!" said Steve, ironically, holding up his shattered niblick. "I like granite, it's so spongy."

"I'm afraid you've got a bad temper, Steve."

But Ventnor had taken out his pipe, lit it and was now doggedly moving toward his ball.

The luck favored him on his next volley, for playing two mid-irons down the hill, he reached the level meadow below safely, while McLemore sliced his second into a row of hot frames, where an indignant horticulturist and two dogs contributed an interesting mental hazard. But the Sphynx handed the farmer a dollar in exchange for lacerated feelings and glass, and the match went on. Over the brook McLemore lay thirteen, having "dubbed" his shot into the stream, but playing steadily after that reached the top of the long hill before them, safely in four more; while Ventnor lost his ball in the bushes and was now playing twenty-five.

CHAPTER XXI

FROM there on, the luck varied and at the Stockbridge farm the score stood McLemore 21; Ventnor, 30. It seemed a difficult lead to overcome, for the Sphynx was playing straight with a mid-iron, while Steve, whose only hope lay in getting distance, had twice pulled into rough grass, which cost him lost balls and extra strokes. The wonder was how he played at all, for Aurora had refused to marry him three times in the last twenty minutes. The result was inevitable, and so like the man in the adage, after playing thirty-eight strokes, he "went up in the air," missing shot after shot and relinquishing all claim to consideration, playing on only because fate seemed to demand it of him.

At the Van Westervelt's fence both men got off "good ones," landing well in the middle of the pasture and had gone forward into the field, their caddies close behind them, when from the shelter of a clump of trees along the stream to their left, there emerged a shadow. Aurora saw it first.

"It's a bull," she said.

"No, it's only a cow," ventured the Sphynx, whose tauric glasses were not adjusted to distances—or to bulls.

"I'm sure it's a bull," repeated Aurora.

Steve glanced at the beast over his shoulder, and then took a brassey from his bag.

"He won't bother us," he muttered. But the animal was approaching majestically, pausing now and then to paw up the dirt with his front hoofs and throwing a cloud of dust over his back.

"It's your parasol, Patty," said Aurora.

"Or Jimmy's vest," put in Patricia.

"You'd better run for it, you and Aurora," said Ventnor. "You can easily make the fence."

"And you?"

"I'm going to play this shot. It's the prettiest lie I've had all day."

"Come, Aurora," said *Patricia*, taking up her bag. "There's no time to lose. He's really coming this way," and gathering up her golf bag and skirts, she ran. The Sphynx, meanwhile, still holding his mid-iron in his hand, was undecided. His ball was twenty yards further on, and his eyes shifted uneasily from the bull to an old apple-tree within a reaching distance. The women by this time had reached a convenient stile and were perched upon it shouting.

"Run, Steve!" they cried. "He's coming!"

Ventnor, who was addressing his ball, glanced up for a moment and then swung. It was the prettiest shot that he had made all day, for the ball started with a low trajectory and soared and soared, clearing the fence on the far side of the field, a carry of two hundred yards, and landed in the next meadow. *T*hen he turned, club in hand, and looked at the bull which now stood twenty paces away, eying them viciously. It was too late to make a sprint for the fence, and like

262

McLemore, Steve wistfully eyed the apple-tree. But he brandished his brassey manfully and prepared to jump aside if the bull lowered his head and rushed him. It was at this moment that Jimmy McLemore, white as a sheet, made up his mind to run. Jimmy's red vest decided the matter, and scorning Ventnor, with a bellow which lent wings to Jimmy's feet, the brute lowered its thick head and charged, passing like a tornado under the limb to which McLemore had fled for safety. Steve Ventnor forgot to be frightened and stood leaning on his club roaring with laughter, for the Sphynx's dignity had always been a fearful and wonderful thing to him. He heard the voices of the women behind him, pleading with him to run, but in his heart Steve Ventnor made a mighty resolution that run he would not. He had no dignity like Jimmy's to lose, but the spectacle Jimmy made decided him. It took some strength of mind to moderate his pace as he picked up Patricia's red parasol and walked toward the fence. The bull however, refused to be distracted, and stood pawing the ground beneath the apple-tree, bellowing up at the soles of the Sphynx's boots and making havoc of the beautiful Campbell mid-iron, which was the only thing of Jimmy's that he could touch.

The women on the stile were laughing, Patricia frankly, uncontrollably, Aurora nervously, looking at Steve as he came up with a queer little anxious wrinkle between her eyebrows.

"I haven't any patience with you," she said. "You might have been gored to death."

Ventnor was still laughing. "I never saw Jimmy run before," he said. "We'll have to get him out of that somehow. I think I'll have a try at it with *Patricia's* parasol."

But *Patricia* quickly snatched it from his hand. Her little drama had worked out far more beautifully than she had ever hoped it would, and she didn't propose to have it ruined now.

"*Nothing* of the sort," she cried. "You may

do whatever you like with your own skin, but that is a perfectly good French parasol, and it's mine." And she put it behind her back.

Meanwhile the Sphynx was pelting the brute below him with apples and shouting anathema, both of which rolled from the animal's impervious back, as he circled angrily around the tree, up which he showed every disposition to climb. From tragic-comedy the scene had degenerated into broadest farce.

"It's like Sothern playing a part of Georgie Coban's," commented *Patricia*, sweetly. "Is he apt to be there all day?"

"It looks so," said Aurora, struggling between anxiety and laughter. "We really ought to do something."

But *Patricia* had settled herself comfortably on the top rail of the fence. *T*hings were going very much to her liking.

"What?" she asked.

"*T*ell somebody. *T*here's a wagon coming this way now."

"But how about the Cross-Country Cup?"

looking at her watch. "There's only an hour and a half to finish in."

"But we can't leave him up there," said Steve, more seriously. "That bull will be there until—until the cows come home."

"Jimmy is perfectly safe," said *Patricia,* "unless he goes to sleep and falls out; and he can't starve unless he throws all the apples at the bull."

"*Patty,* you're heartless," said Aurora, but she laughed when she said it.

The farmer who came along in the wagon took in the situation at a glance and laughing more loudly than any of them, consented at last to drive to the barnyard and tell the farmer.

"It won't do any good," he said, sagely. "That bull won't go back until he follows the cows at milking time. He might quit before that—I dunno. I'll do what I can though." And with a laconic chirrup to his nag, he departed in the direction of the Van Westervelts' farmyard.

The party of three followed him with their eyes until he had disappeared in a cloud of dust and then examined the apple-tree from which the Sphynx's legs dangled hopelessly. The rest of him was hidden among the leaves.

"Until the cows come home," said *Patricia*, solemnly, and looking into one another's eyes all three of them burst into shameless laughter. And with that laugh free-masonry was established. It was plainly to be read in Aurora's eyes. The toppling of Jimmy's dignity had been too much for her own sense of gravity.

Patricia meanwhile had taken out her watch. "*T*his, my dear children," she said, indicating with a fine gesture, the Sphynx's apple-tree, "is one of the hazards of the *N*ew Game of Golf. *T*here is only an hour and a half to finish in. *P*lay the game, you two, I must wait."

"It wouldn't be the sporting thing," said Steve, struggling with a desire to obey.

"I'd like to know who is as good a judge

of the rules of a game as its inventor," said
Patricia. "Am I right, Aurora?"

Aurora by this time was fingering at the
strap of Ventnor's golf bag. "Yes," she decided, "as *Patricia* says, it's in the game."

Steve glanced at her quickly, joyfully, but
her head was lowered and she was already
down the steps of the stile and walking along
the road toward the adjoining meadow. Ventnor's eyes met *Patricia's* for the fraction of a
second of wireless telegraphy, after which
Steve plunged down the steps and followed
his caddy.

The gabled roof of Augustus *N*orth's house
was visible above the trees scarcely half a
mile away, but the paper chase led to it by
devious, sequestered ways, which Steve Ventnor and his caddy scrupulously followed.
Many times on the way they stopped in the
shadow of the trees, and but a few minutes of
time remained when Steve ran down his putt.
It had taken him just one hundred and three
shots to do that last nine hundred yards in an

hour and forty minutes. His caddy counted them; which only went to prove her a conscientious person, for under the circumstances book-keeping was a difficult matter.

*P*erched upon her stile, in smiling patience *Patricia* waited "until the cows came home," while Mortimer Crabb, who had been notified over the telephone of the disaster, drove up to see the final chapter in Jimmy McLemore's undoing. For the farmer came and at some pains extracted him from his perilous post. The Crabbs drove McLemore to his home in their motor and then ran over to the *N*orths to hear how the cross-country match had finished, The happy couple met them at the steps.

"The ball is in the hole, *Patty*, dear," said Steve Ventnor. "Do I win the Cup?"

"You do," said *Patricia*, looking at her watch, "by three hours and a half. And it's a loving-cup, Steve, with cupids and things, I had it made especially for you and Aurora."

Aurora kissed *Patricia* with enthusiasm.

"How did you know, *Patty*, it was to be Steve?"

"Simplest thing imaginable! Because Steve is the most adorable boy, always excepting Mort, that was ever born—and then you know, Aurora—you couldn't have married Jimmy!"

"*That's* true," said Aurora, thinking of Jimmy's legs in the apple-tree, "I really couldn't."

Steve refused to return to the Crabbs' to dinner, so the Makers of Opportunities departed alone. Mortimer drove slowly through the gathering dusk and *Patricia* sat silent.

"Are you happy, *Patty*?" he asked, at last.

"No, of course not," said *Patricia*, pinching his ear, "you know I'm never happy with you, Mort."

"Aren't you getting a little tired of putting the world in order?"

"Oh, yes. But young people are *so* provoking. *They* can never make up their own minds, and you know *somebody* has to do it for them."

"Haven't you ever wondered how the world would get on without you?"

"*No*, but sometimes I've wondered how you would."

"I? Ah! I wouldn't get on at all. And yet you know there's a responsibility in being married to a Dea ex Machina."

"What, please?"

"The machinery may run down."

"And then?"

"The goddess may end in the ditch."

"Mort!"

"Or get a blow-out—you came near it, *Patty*."

"I didn't, Mort—ever."

"How about——?"

He was going to say John Doe, but she put her fingers over his lips so that he only mumbled.

"*No*, Mort—I'm a prudent goddess—a chauffeuse extraordinary."

"I'm sure of that, but——"

"But what?"

"No car can endure so long out of the garage."

"You're a silly old thing." She sighed comfortably and leaned her head over on his shoulder. In a moment she spoke again. "I think you're quite right though, Mort."

"Aren't you tired of making opportunities for other people?"

She made a sound that he understood.

"I am, a little, you know, *Patty*," he added. The motor purred gently as it glided out of a country road into the turnpike.

"What do you say if we begin making opportunities for each other?"

She started up with a laugh.

"I never thought of that," she said. "When shall we start?"

"At once, *Patty*. If you'll provide the opportunity," and he kissed her, "I'll be its thief."

But she captured him at once.

THE END.   (1)

Mrs. Thompson

The story deals with a woman who had won for herself an enviable position in the business world, when she is persuaded to marry one of her employees, who turns out to be an adventurer. Her disappointment strengthens her already wonderfully strong character, and the outcome of the story is as amazing as it is unusual.

12mo. Cloth, $1.30 net.

The Rest Cure

The story of a husband who is absolutely wrapped up in his business, devotes all his days and nights to it, allows his wife to do as she likes. She looks about for other companionship; suddenly they both wake up to the situation that the husband is ruining his life by his work and that the wife is ruining herself through lack of companionship with her husband.

" The book grips like a steel trap, and only the stupid could read it unmoved."—*Chicago Record-Herald.*

12mo. Cloth, $1.50 net.

Seymour Charlton

The story of the love and marriage of a young English earl and the daughter of a shopkeeper. She does not at first succeed in her new position. Later, however, she becomes a great lady in every sense of the word, only to discover that her husband has become entangled with a woman of a fast life. Charlton's tardy recognition of his wife's worth meets no response from her. But having finally broken with the other woman, he starts in all over again to win his wife's love.

Illustrated. 12mo. Cloth, $1.50.

The Guarded Flame

"In quite a different field, in a vastly different atmosphere, the author has come near to the master genius of Thomas Hardy. 'The Guarded Flame' is a work of wonderful power, but above all a work of truth. No novel has been written since the beginning of Hardy's literary activity that has more clearly approached his marvelous subtlety in the depiction of human nature."—*The Cleveland Plain Dealer.*

12mo. Cloth, $1.50.

Vivien

This story gives the detailed experiences of a girl who has to fight single-handed against the greatest dangers to which a woman can be exposed and to see sides of life of which her more fortunate sisters are kept in ignorance. It is fascinatingly written and with a clear understanding of human nature.

12mo. Cloth, $1.50.

D. APPLETON AND COMPANY
NEW YORK   LONDON

By ELINOR GLYN

His Hour

The story of the loves of a Russian Prince and a beautiful Englishwoman by the author of "Three Weeks." With frontispiece. 12mo. Cloth, $1.50.

A young English widow of wealth and position traveling in Egypt meets a Russian prince of great personal charm and high rank, whose masterful attentions at once pique the lady's warm interest. They are companions on her return voyage to England, during which her emotions are further stirred by the varied characteristics of the young prince, and almost immediately she leaves for St. Petersburg to visit her godmother, a woman of rank and fashion, whom she had hitherto never met. In St. Petersburg she again meets the young prince, who is a great favorite. Love between them develops, but the man's assurance and frank expectations render the lady haughty and reserved. There are occasions, however, when she yields to his ardor in so far as to show that she loves him. From this point the author then spins a vivid and exotic love story, and one that will appeal to all classes of fiction readers.

"A tale that many will read with bated breath."
—*New York Herald.*

"The wild nature of the Russian prince, as well as the charmingly free and easy society of St. Petersburg, are admirably drawn."
—*Philadelphia Public Ledger.*

D. APPLETON & COMPANY, NEW YORK

Lightning Source UK Ltd.
Milton Keynes UK
UKHW011259070119
335137UK00016B/1260/P

9 781331 357674